GRIFFIN HAYES

I0620405

NIGHTFALL

A
COLLECTION
OF
DARK TALES

Trebor Books

TREBOR BOOKS

ISBN: 978-0-9918881-0-8

Cover design by Griffin Hayes
Edited by Andrea Harding

Also by Griffin Hayes

Novels
Malice
Dark Passage

Novellas
Hive I
Hive II
Hive III
Bird of Prey
The Neighbors

Short Stories
The Second Coming
The Grip
Fatherland

Collections
Night Terror
Nightfall

Contents

Foreword

The night has always been a particularly frightening time of the day for me. I can remember running up the stairs to my bedroom as a teenager, growing quite certain that ghostly hands were reaching out from the darkness to grab hold of my ankles. Not long after that, I grew convinced that Freddy Kruger was hiding in my closet, waiting for me to fall asleep. I guess you could say I've been living in fear for a long time and in a way, the stories you're about to read were my way of exorcising that terror. But fear of the dark isn't anything new. It's been around since the dawn of mankind and it'll probably stay with us, in one form or another, forever. Perhaps the best anyone can hope for is to stare it flat in the face and hope you don't blink. Blinking would be bad, because whatever's lurking in the darkness can smell fear the way that sharks can smell blood. So take my hand now and come peer with me into the darkness. Take a deep breath. Give your eyes some time to adjust. Just remember, if you see something strange shambling through the darkness: don't blink.

Note: I've included some background for all of the stories included in this collection and placed them either before or after the story in question. For the most part, these are simply my inspiration for each tale and why I'd been eager to explore a particular subject. I know these sorts of things appeal mostly to writers, so I encourage most readers to skip them entirely. The stories are all meant to be stand-alone explorations of different inspirations.

Cheers,
Griffin Hayes

BIRD OF PREY

I wrote Bird of Prey after Last Call—you'll only understand the significance of that once you've read both stories (it's last). Around that time, I'd been doing a lot of reading on the Mothman legend. I watched a few documentaries, saw The Mothman Prophecies, which frankly creeped the shit out of me, and felt like this might be the thing I'd tackle next. After my subconscious mulled it over for a few days, a handful of 'what ifs' started popping up. What if the Mothman wasn't a single creature, but a species? What if they bred, once every hundred years and then descended on the closest town, to feed? I was already getting excited. Gradually, during the writing, the creature became less moth and more bird-like. I also grew to love the four unlikely men who felt obliged to head into that abandoned steel works in order to save their town.

Part 1

Tommy 'The Tank' Hodgkins skidded his Firebird into
Lucky Lonie's parking lot, going about twenty miles an
hour faster than he really should have been. The Bird's
tires locked in a high c before they kicked up a thick,
rubbery cloud of smoke.

Buck Sanders was pacing back and forth out in front
of Lonie's, oblivious to the fact that Tommy had nearly
sent him careening over the hood, off the windshield and
into a thicket of Yellow Cedar.

A shaft of sunlight come down through the trees,
illuminating Buck like a spotlight. Tommy could see that
the sign on the door of the bar was flipped to CLOSED.
Buck's balding head was slick with sweat. Three
mosquitoes were sucking away merrily at his skull. A
surprising sight since Buck was a man who took immense
pleasure in squashing those 'little bastards' whenever he
could.

Buck came to the open window.

"So where is this thing?" Tommy asked.

"Stay right there, we're going to Keisel's."

There was a blood stained hanky wrapped around
Buck's left hand.

"The Keisel steel factory?" Tommy asked. "What on
Earth for? It's abandoned."

Buck threw him the look that people throw when they're not in the mood to repeat themselves and crossed to the passenger side door before climbing inside, mosquitoes and all.

"Take the A3," Buck began, pulling a hand across his forehead and wiping it on the leg of his jeans. "It's quicker. Get off just before Harmond Avenue and hang three rights. Steel Works is a big bitch, can't miss her."

Tommy pulled out and headed for the A3.

"That where you left it?" Tommy finally inquired when they hit the interstate. He could practically see the whirlwind of thoughts tussling around inside Buck's head. Buck nodded absently.

"Buck, I gotta ask. What in hell's name were you doing over there in the first place?"

"The leak was getting real bad …"

"Huh?"

"I was gone to get siding to fix the leak in the roof."

Lonie's was certainly no Taj Mahal; this Tommy knew without a doubt, but metal siding, ripped from an abandoned steel factory? The bar was already on its way to looking like something out of a 1930's shanty town, it sure as hell didn't need any help.

"Buck, I've never seen you like this, in all the time I've known you."

Buck looked at him and then fell into a moody silence, his face the color of raw chicken. Something had the old man scared bad.

When Tommy wasn't tending bar at Lonie's, he and Buck were usually out hunting or dreaming up quick and easy ways to strike it rich. But in all the time they had known each other, the strangest thing they had ever come across was a five legged deer: nothing any self-respecting cryptozoologist would even blink twice at. And they had even let the deer amble back into the thick brush that day, partly because, as Buck had put it, 'when mother

3

nature fucks up that bad, it's best to leave the poor thing be; she'll have a hard enough time getting on without two yahoos trying to blast her to bits.'

The sudden sound of Buck's voice startled Tommy. "First time I seen the thing, I didn't think much of it. Looked to me like one of them birds … like an eagle. Wingspan eight, maybe nine feet. And it was circlin' overhead, right above me, the way eagles tend to when they're lookin' for somethin' to eat."

"No shortage of rats at Keisel's," Tommy said, "that's for sure."

Buck glared at him with frightening intensity. "Damn right! And that's when it hit me that something was wrong. Where the heck were the other birds? I mean, I can't remember ever seeing less than a dozen bald eagles flyin' over the steel works."

Tommy exited the A3 and made a right.

"At the time," Buck said, "I tried not to give it too much thought. Jesus, I'm no small man, Tommy." Buck's forearms were flexing almost on cue, the muscles in his arms bunching up like taught cords. "There's not a lot of worrying needs to be done when a bird looks like its eyeing me for dinner. Matter of fact, at the time I was sure it was lookin' for something else, like some dumb squirrel that had got its head stuck in a hole somewhere.

"So I got my crowbar with me and I'm jimmying a nice piece of paneling off one of those small depot sheds, when my hand slips and I slice a strip the size of Bethany Elroy's ass crack." Buck held the outer edge of his left hand in the air. The blood-stained hanky fluttered into his lap. It looked to Tommy like a shrapnel wound from one of those fancy Hollywood war movies: a jagged and meaty gash, dripping red. But there was something else there as well. Something that made Tommy's mouth go dry. Stitched in a crescent pattern, on the back of Buck's hand and across his palm, was a set of teeth marks. At least they looked like teeth marks, but they weren't from any set of jaws Tommy had ever seen. Hundreds of tiny pinpricks, set neatly in a curved line.

"Buck, your hand!" Tommy's attention snapped back to the road and he realized with a jolt of panic he had wandered over into the oncoming lane. The tires squealed as he veered back.

Buck studied his hand, turning it over in his lap as though he were trying on a pair of expensive gloves. "It was right after I sliced her open that I heard this scream, high pitched like a woman's scream, but from far away and when I looked up, that thing was diving down at me, wings folded, eyes blazing. Two blood red chili peppers is what they looked like. There was something cold about them. Something prehistoric." Buck drew a fresh hanky out of his back pocket and held it against the wound. "It was the blood, Tommy. I didn't realize at the time, but it was the blood that it smelled."

"Like a shark," Tommy said, suddenly not feeling so sure about what he was getting himself into.

"Truth be told, I wanted to run. I won't bullshit you, Tommy. We've known each other too long for that. I wanted to run so bad I could feel my legs twitching under me, but it felt like one of those dreams, where your legs are pumping like hell but you're not going anywhere. I'm telling you this, Tommy, cause I trust you'll never breathe a goddamn word of it to anyone, so long as you live. But facts are facts and the fact is, I nearly crapped in my pants. Happened so fast too, only real memory I have is putting my arm into the air, like for protection. And then it slammed into me, latching onto my arm, sending me ass backwards into the dirt." Buck looked down at his hand.

"Those fingers it had were long and thin with pointed claws and its feet were just the same, like one of those orangutans. And all over its body were wispy gray

5

feathers … and the smell. God awful. Like when they found Jed Peterson in his favorite recliner, dead nearly a month, maggots crawling all over his face."

Tommy could feel Buck's eyes boring into him. "But it was the mouth that I remember most …"

Tommy made another right and in the distance he could see the very tip of the abandoned Keisel steel factory, looming above the tree tops. His eyes made a quick scan, but the sky above it seemed empty.

Buck followed Tommy's eyes and then dropped them back to his throbbing hand. "That's when it bit me. And I'll guarantee, you've never felt pain like that in your life. Like a thousand tetanus shots all at once. Its jaw latched on as if I was holding a piece of steak out to a vulture. I screamed, Tommy. I'm not afraid to admit that. Maybe for the first time since I was a little pissant in diapers, I screamed and I wasn't gonna stop until I felt the cold steel of that crowbar still in my other hand and I brought it down as hard as I could. I was aiming for the thing's head you see, but you have to understand, it didn't really have a head, not like you or I, at least. Its head came out of its shoulders, almost like a moth. Hell, a lot like a moth. A giant moth with red eyes and two sets of hands."

Part II
'Introductions All Around'

The Keisel Steel Works' main building looked like a red barn on steroids. It rose nearly two hundred feet into the sky. Six smoke stacks jutted from the roof in a neat line. Around the main building were a collection of hodgepodge structures, some of them large enough to park a fleet of Buick Eldorados in, others no bigger than an outhouse, and yet everything here bore the unmistakable aura of decay. Seventy brutal Alaska winters had a nasty habit of doing that to a place. Tommy and Buck walked along a gravel path strewn with debris; bits of rusted piping, metal girders discarded railway ties. There was even a porcelain toilet propped up against a wall, a healthy crack right down the middle.

Buck raised his hand, the one wrapped in the bloodied hanky and pointed straight ahead. In the distance, Tommy could see the depot shed with a patch of side paneling that looked as though someone had been yanking at it. That was Buck's handy work.

"You're sure it was dead, right?" Tommy asked, trying to ignore the squeak in his voice.

"I can guarantee you I bashed its head in with a cinder block. Trust me, it's deader'n a doornail."

A minute later they arrived at the shed. On a patch of yellowing grass was a cinderblock, caked and crusted in blood, just like Buck had said. On the metal siding, a thin red line ran down one of the grooves. The place where Buck had cut himself. Again, just like he had said. But the creature he had described was nowhere to be found.

Tommy looked over at Buck. The stunned look on the old man's face slowly twisted into alarm.

"There's no way it could have survived that …" Buck was mumbling as he scanned the ground for a trail of blood but found none. Neither did Tommy. He was about to suggest that they should split up and search for wherever it might have disappeared to, when something far above them blocked out the sun. A cloud had passed over. At least that was Tommy's first thought, but deep down he knew that clouds didn't make sounds like the one he had just heard. Clouds didn't sound like industrial sized fans, pushing at the air in great swoops. Both men looked up into the sky, blinking at the sun, and it was then, at nearly the same instant, that their jaws fell open.

What had blocked out the light was no passing cloud, no Jumbo Jet flying far overhead, but rather the wings of something that defied logic. Tommy tried to speak, but his mouth felt as if it had been filled with a bucket of hot sand. Beside him, Buck's chapped lips formed a perfect 'O'. For a moment, they stood at attention, watching as something inexplicable circled overhead.

Tommy spoke first. "You seeing what I'm seeing? Wingspan's gotta be nearly thirty feet. Oh God, Buck, what is that? What is that damned thing Buck? Buck, what in sweet he…"

Buck grabbed the meat on the back of Tommy's arm and squeezed as hard as he could. Tommy yanked free with a yelp and for another timeless second both men stood staring at each other, the same thought telegraphed on their faces: "Run!"

Tommy looked down and as if in slow motion saw the blood dripping from Buck's hand. A small puddle had collected in the gravel by his feet. A terrifying thought struck him with the force of a hurricane: he was thinking of the great white shark again. No sooner had this thought begun to solidify than it was drowned out by the shriek, a nerve shattering sound so loud it sent the hairs on the back of their respective necks straight up. When Tommy looked up again, the creature had already begun to dive.

Both men spun on their heels. The car couldn't have been more than a hundred yards away; at that moment it felt like the furthest hundred yards they'd navigated in their lives. They were two men who, in all their collective years, had never backed down from a single fight. Two men who could hold their own in any circumstances. Two men, running with everything they had.

● ● ●

Tommy was the first to fall. He tripped over a rusted metal pipe and went sprawling onto the gravel path, arms stretched out like Superman. The flapping behind him had become deafening. Whoomp! Whoomp! Whoomp!

He didn't dare look back, especially when he saw the expression on Buck's face ahead of him when he glanced over his shoulder. The old man's face had turned the color of sour milk. Tommy scrambled to his feet and it was then that he felt an intense rush of air and claws grasping for purchase. Something closed around his shoulder like a vice and lifted him up off the ground. Eddies of powerful wind ripped holes into the gravel path. Tommy threw back his head and when he saw the thing up close, the pain in his shoulder seemed to evaporate. Above him was a great coat of matted gray fur, whipping around in the wind, stinking something awful. Twigs and dried leaves covered its underbelly as though it

9

had been scouring the forest floor when it smelled them coming. When it craned its head down, perhaps to see what prize it had won, its blood red slits found Tommy, and it fixed him with a glare that felt to Tommy like he had just met the devil himself.

Then came the explosion of pain and with it the realization that if he let this thing carry him off, he was a goner. He reached for his shoulder and grasped one of the leathery talons buried into his flesh and bent it back until he heard the unmistakable sound of snapping bone. The creature's grip loosened at once and Tommy fell nearly fifteen feet, arms and legs reeling madly. He landed with a thud on a patch of soft ground beside the path, the tumble enough to rattle every bone in his body. He rolled a handful of times before scrambling to his feet.

Buck was the next to fall. He had been looking over his shoulder, watching as the creature with the wispy gray fur and the pointed claws had swooped down and plucked Tommy up like an empty beer can. A big part of him had wanted to stop and help Tommy, but whatever aspect of his brain was now in control had pulled an emergency shutdown and refused to take orders. Tommy was five feet in the air when Buck went face first into the gravel. There was a searing stab of pain as his bloody hand was raked over the sharp stones. The hanky had been torn off on impact and now his wound was caked with bits of dirt and rubble.

The object that had snagged Buck's foot hadn't been some rusted pipe or open toilet seat. It had been a human leg, sticking out from the bushes. The body was badly mangled, almost unrecognizable. Almost. But Buck knew right away who it was. Fast Eddy Fick, the hermit who lived in the woods over by Fay's Crossing. Buck couldn't tell from the face, of course, since that was little more than a bloody pulp, but he knew by the shredded tan winter coat and the billy boots. The same clothes Fast Eddy had probably worn every day for the last fifteen years. The body lay face down, arms up over its head as though the man had died trying to protect his face.

Buck scrambled to his feet. Tommy was ahead of him now, free from the creature's grip, his legs pumping for the car like it was the all-state finals. The right shoulder of his checkered shirt was torn and bloody.

Buck looked skyward and saw the thing push off with its giant, leathery wings. It rose into the air sharply and then barrel rolled like one of those old WWI fighter planes. It was circling back for another go at them. Even at that distance, he could make out those two red eyes, the size of footballs, glaring down at him.

Tommy was at the car when he turned around and saw it diving for Buck. There was forty yards between Buck and the car; he could tell by the old man's glistening face, he wasn't going to make it. Tommy slid into the driver's seat and fumbled in his pockets for the keys, only dimly aware of the pain in his shoulder. "Come on you whore! Where are you?" Left pocket … his trembling hand slipped in and found nothing. Right pocket … Tommy's fingers hit a familiar piece of serrated metal. He pulled out the key and shoved it into the ignition, turning until his ears registered what had to be the most beautiful sound he had ever heard; the Firebird coughing to life. He leaned over to prop the passenger side door open and punched the accelerator.

The female shriek pierced the air again, louder this time; it sounded pissed.

Tommy looked up and saw that it was nearly on Buck. The panic on the old man's face was absolute. That clawing feeling that something is closing fast and you can't look back, can't look back or it's over.

Buck did what was perhaps the only intelligent thing he could under the circumstances: he skidded to a stop,

11

spun around, and started running in the opposite direction. The angle was too steep for the creature to change its trajectory and it disengaged, whipping back up into the sky. Tommy pulled up alongside Buck and the older man jumped in. Tommy jerked the wheel and spun the car around to face the outbound road. Tommy punched the Firebird's accelerator and a stream of gravel kicked up as the car accelerated. A single thought was ringing through Tommy's head:

This is mission control, we have lift-off!

Buck was in the passenger seat, wheezing and coughing up yellow gobs of phlegm. He looked over at Tommy's shoulder.

"Jesus Christ," he said, pulling off his own shirt and tearing a strip off to use as a tourniquet.

Buck peered out of the rear window. He had hoped to see the creature circling over the steel works and he panicked for a moment; it was nowhere to be found.

Maybe it was over the car.

But then he spotted it over Keisel's, little more than an indistinguishable grayish form. It swooped down and landed on the roof by one of the smoke stacks and ambled into a hole and out of sight.

Like a fucking bird heading back to its nest, Buck thought to himself.

Tommy angled his wounded shoulder out of his shirt and surveyed the damage. There were two puncture holes, the size of silver dollars, one beside his pectoral muscle and the other behind his shoulder blade. Buck wrapped his torn shirt over the wound and under Tommy's arm, tying it in a sailor's knot to keep it from coming undone.

"There's no way in Sam Hill that was the one you killed, Buck, no fucking way."

"Don't you think I know that?" Buck snapped, fighting to examine his handiwork in the bucking car.

"Compared to that bitch, what I got seemed more like … a baby."

Tommy shot him a wide-eyed glance.

What Buck said next came out more smoothly than he had meant it to. "I think we just met Mama."

The implication took a moment to sink in.

"So there could be dozens of those things flying around? What if they get someone else …?" Buck looked away. "What? What is it Buck? What is it that you know?"

"Fast Eddy Fick. At least what was left of him, half sticking out of the bushes."

"Oh Christ! We gotta call the sheriff."

"And tell him a giant bird ate Fast Eddy's face off and then took you for a joy ride? Come on, Tommy! By the time those chowder heads get their act together, who knows how many others are—"

"Then what? We can't just pretend none of this happened." There was a touch of desperation in Tommy's voice. "You said yourself that when mother nature goofs…"

"I know what I said," Buck cut in. His wound was still bleeding. "A five-legged deer, that's a goof, no question. But that thing up there is no run of the mill goof; it's a bloody monstrosity and it needs to be wiped off the face of the earth … before it gets hungry for something other than stringy old hermits." He paused. "Before it moves into town."

Tommy looked pensive. A bead of sweat rolled down his face and onto his jeans, forming a dark blue dot. He looked over at Buck. "We're gonna need some help. And guns, lots of guns."

Part III
'The Beast's Handiwork'

What Tommy hadn't counted on, was the reaction they got from Tig and Allan; both regulars at Lonie's, who had arrived less than an hour after Buckcalled them. Tommy had figured that once the snickers and cajoling were out of the way, they might get down to discussing the business of how best to kill the thing at Keisel's. But there was no cajoling and nothing even remotely resembling a snicker. Tig Kowski and Allan Racine had fallen into a dead silence at the first mention of the birdman. The muscles in Tig's narrow jaw had been noticeably clenched and when the lanky man swallowed, his Adam's apple had poked out from his pencil thin neck had bobbed like a fishing pole.

Allan's reaction might have been the same, except the pudginess that Buck liked to call the man's 'baby fat' had only allowed the folds of his neck to quiver ever so slightly.

Something about the uneasy expression on Tig's face worried Tommy. It was more than the kind of fearful look one would expect; there was terror in the man's eyes. Above all, there was recognition.

"Tig ..." Tommy began.

But Tig never let him finish.

"My great-granddaddy lived to be an old man," Tig said. "Ninety-eight years old, nearly. Years ago, he used to tell about something he had seen when he was just a kid. Said his ma had told him to go fetch the clothes off the drying line and that he'd gone out in the middle of a bright, sunny day and no sooner had he grabbed hold of his first bed sheet, than the sky had turned as black as night. Said he'd looked up thinking a big black cloud had come overhead and could barely believe his eyes when he'd seen thousands of birds—'dihnasores' he called them—flying toward Drexel. He'd never seen anything like it again, he said, until WWII when all those planes took to the sky for D-Day."

"Where's Drexel?" Tommy asked. "I've never heard of it."

"Course you haven't," Tig replied. "Drexel went from being one of the biggest Alaskan logging towns to little more than a vacant lot, with busted out buildings. As if everyone had just picked up and ran away. Except no one ever left Drexel. Damned eeriest thing he'd ever seen, my grandfather said."

"I don't understand," Tommy said sounding exasperated. "What's the point of wiping out a whole town?"

Allan flicked the ash off his cigarette with one of his pudgy fingers. "You said this thing was part man and part moth?"

Buck nodded. "We did."

"Any of youse ever heard of the Winter Moth?"

No one said anything. Their collective expressions said they didn't have patience for one of Allan's stories.

"A cousin of mine down in Massachusetts that told me 'bout it last year. I guess by its name you wouldn't think much. Winter Moth. Giddy up, right? But when March comes rolling along and those larvae start

15

hatching, hell, they've been known to strip entire neighborhoods of every leaf they ever had."

There was an audible click in Tig's throat.

"How long do you think we have?" Tommy asked.

Allan took a final drag of his cigarette and then stubbed it out between yellowed fingers. "Hard to say. It may already be too late."

Buck's face was nearly expressionless. A sort of morbid determination had come over him. Both his and Tommy's wounds continued to bleed and for some inexplicable reason, a growing part of Tommy suspected that bleeding wouldn't stop until the creature and its offspring were destroyed.

Buck reached under the bar and produced a sawed-off shotgun. His initials were carved into the chestnut stock: B.S.

Tommy stood beside him, the handle of a gun poking out the front of his jeans. He removed it and laid it on the table. The gun was a Colt .45. Eight-shot magazine—a respectable firearm with a large slow moving bullet capable of knocking a grown man off his feet. A look of surprise came across Buck's face when the gun came out. "I keep it strapped under the Bird's front seat," Tommy explained, a little sheepishly. "You never know when you're gonna need a little firepower."

Buck looked over at the two men. "Let's see what you brought."

Tig and Allan nodded and each picked up the long black cases resting at their feet. To the casual observer it might have seemed the men were getting ready for a friendly game of eight ball. Tig laid his case on the edge of the oak table and undid the zipper. His hand disappeared inside and he came out with a Winchester 94. It looked like something from an old John Wayne western. That Tig and guns did not get along; it was especially obvious by the way he grasped the rifle by the barrel instead of the stock. Tig wasn't much for hunting either, but that was more because in Tig's opinion, fiddling around with guns in the woods had a nasty habit of eating into the time he could spend drunk at Lonie's. In truth, the gun was a gift from a distant uncle who happened to be a self-described gun nut. An uncle who had never liked Tig and was hell bent on sticking his 'good for nothing' nephew with something he would never have a use for.

A look of triumph had spread steadily across Tig's face as that gun had come out and Tommy suspected it had more to do with proving his uncle wrong than the pleasure of handling such a fine weapon.

"And the other stuff I asked you to bring?" Buck asked.

Tig produced a large blue duffel bag from under his chair and unzipped it. Inside were miner's helmets. Tig reached in carefully and removed a shoebox tied with bungee cords. He opened the box and pulled out ten sticks of dynamite, lashed together with a timer.

Tommy's eyes went wide. "Gezuz, Buck, what's the idea? We're going to shoot the bloody things, not blow the whole fucking metal works sky high."

"Oh really?" Buck shot back. "And what if there are more of those damn things than we have bullets for? What then?"

Buck was right and Tommy knew it.

"That place is gonna be crawling with those things and you and I both know it. We can't afford to let a single one get out."

The three of them looked at Allan.

Allan undid his case next.

Tommy stifled a nervous laugh when he saw what the fat man had brought with him. A five-shot Springfield rifle from WWI. A bloody bolt-action. The expression on Allan's face reflected that he could feel the mood in the

17

room souring. "Guys, this was all I could get at such short notice," he squealed defensively. "Ma almost wouldn't let me have it. She was real crabby this morning. I had to promise her I'd re-shingle the roof."

The weathered features on Buck's face hardened. "I'm not happy, Allan. Serious, reliable firepower was what I asked you to bring and you show up with an antique piece of shit. I'll say it again, I ain't happy. But we ain't got the luxury of being angry right now. And we ain't got time to run down to Jerry's Gunmart and start shoppin' around. If Tig's story about Drexel is true and these things intend to swoop in and carry off everyone we know, then there ain't any other choice but to blow them the fuck up."

Buck's eyes dropped to the case in front of Allan. "Now. How many shells you got?"

The color that rose in Allan's face gave Tommy butterflies.

"Thirty …" And as the words hit the air, Allan's eyes dropped. For a frantic moment they darted between a half-empty pack of matches next to an overflowing ashtray and a broken beer glass, lying forgotten under the table. "Maybe twelve."

Buck's mouth dropped open, as though he were about to unload a can and a half of verbal whoop ass, when the phone behind the bar began to ring. On the third ring, Buck's mouth tightened into a grimace and he left to answer it.

"Lonie's," he snapped and then paused briefly. "Speaking. What is it?"

A strained expression fell over Buck's face. All three men studied him intently. Then his expression shifted to something that resembled dread, and then anger. He shook his head, mumbled something Tommy and the others couldn't quite hear and hung up the phone.

Tommy stepped forward "What is it?"

"That was Bobby Miller."

Tig's eyebrows went up. "Deputy Miller? What'd he want?"

Buck's hand reached for the wet rag by the sink and wrung it dry. "Said for over an hour now, he's been flooded with all kinds of weird calls. Old couple on the edge of town said they seen something strange. Like a giant man with wings. Asked if I'd seen anything strange myself."

Buck's eyes had glazed over. "If it wasn't for me, none of this would be happening."

"You heard Tig's story, Buck," Tommy was saying. "It was just a matter of time before they came snoopin' around. For all we know, Fast Eddy'd been dead for days." He made his way to the bar, but Buck wasn't buying a single word of it. The only thing worse than Buck's short temper was his stubbornness.

"Get your gear," Buck barked. "We're headin' out."

Tommy stuffed the .45 into the seat of his pants. Tig and Allan shouldered their rifles and filled their pockets with what few bullets they had.

The three of them waited in the car for Buck. When he finally reappeared, he was carrying the blue duffel bag.

A thick layer of sweat and grease glistened on Allan's forehead.

"Pop the trunk, will ya?" Buck told Tommy.

Tommy did as he asked and Allan squeezed his head out the window. A stiff breeze came through the pines and flipped a tuft of thinning hair into his cherubic face. "Seriously Buck, let's not go gettin' ourselves blown up."

Buck turned to him. "Just stay close when the shit hits the fan, and you'll be fine." He slid into the car. "Let's roll."

• • •

They came upon a Plymouth Voyager with Oregon plates about a mile from Keisel's.

Above the trees, the line of smoke stacks was clearly visible and whenever Tommy found himself glancing up at the empty sky above the place, the palms of his hands would fill with sweat. The late afternoon sun was low and in their eyes, turning the sky the color of an overripe peach. He knew that the chances of seeing the thing hovering, waiting for them, were next to nil. But no matter how much sense it made, that kind of thinking didn't make one bit of difference. His eyes still searched the sky.

The blinding sun meant that they didn't really get a good look at the minivan until they were almost up its ass. It was splayed across the road, the passenger side door ajar. A leg with a white tennis shoe was peeking out. The normality of it made Tommy uneasy. But it wasn't as normal as it at first appeared. Even from their vehicle, they could see that the roof was torn open and peeled back, like a can of sardines.

In the back seat of the Firebird, Allan fumbled as he tried loading the five-shot clip into his Springfield. Three bullets tumbled from his hands and spilled to the ground, bouncing around his feet. He let out a billowing sigh; his breath was heavy and sour.

Tommy opened his door and stepped out. His hand closed around the .45 tucked into his pants. He pulled back on the slide and the gun made a clicking sound. A red handprint was smeared down the driver's side window. Suddenly, gun or no gun, all the moisture suddenly went out of Tommy's mouth.

Buck was also out of the Firebird and heading for the passenger door. Tig and Allan were in the rear, each with a leg in the Bird and one on the dirt road. Buck turned slowly and looked back at them. The index and second fingers of his right hand rose in a V to his eyes and then pointed upwards.

They got the message and scanned the sky so the birdman wouldn't catch them out in the open with their pants down. Not again, at least.

It didn't take long for Tommy to discover there was little sense in trying to peer in through the tinted back windows. He sidled up next to the front door and saw a body, lying face down against the steering wheel. He popped the driver's side door open and the smell that spilled out reminded him of the butcher shop down on Easton Avenue. A stench strong enough to make you think you were chewing on a mouthful of rusty nails. Tommy tugged the body of a man. It slumped into the seat with a wet slap. The guy's scalp had been peeled open and rolled back—like the roof. And it was clear by the positioning of the woman's body on the passenger side—her door open and a single foot poking out—that the paralyzing effects of fear had released their hold too late.

In the back, Buck found a baby seat and a cheap imitation Barbie doll, signs that children had once been back there, but not any longer.

"She's going after kids," Tommy said in horror.

A stuffed dog stared back at him, blood smeared across its furry face.

Flies had ventured in through the open roof and were buzzing happily around the gore that had once been a man's head.

Buck did not reply right away.

Tommy removed the hand that was covering his mouth. "Buck, she's taken the kids! They may still be—"

"The kids are dead," Buck said matter of factly. The words came out so coldly that it frightened Tommy. "My

21

guess is it won't be long before she's back for these two either."

A kind of calmness had come over Buck, the way it does when a man decides he's had enough of life. Maybe it was the guilt he was feeling at the thought of the sky, thick with those things. Tommy was becoming more certain every minute that a belief had taken hold of Buck; a belief that in some way he had started this whole mess. The look was one Tommy had seen before and a chilling certainty came over him that these killings would end tonight. They would end, or Buck would die trying.

● ● ●

They arrived at the steel works ten minutes later. An unnerving tranquility had settled over the area. Every wild creature within a square mile seemed to have disappeared. Almost every one.

Guns and blue duffel bag in hand, the four men followed the gravel path toward the main building— toward the hole in the roof that Buck had seen that thing disappear into, not two hours before. Along the way, they came to the spot where Buck had found Fast Eddy Fick, lying on the ground with his face all shredded. The gravel was disturbed where Buck had taken his spill, but as the two men had secretly feared, Eddie's body had gone. What really made the color drain from Tommy's face ,however, was the way the blood had also vanished— every last drop of it -as though an army of bloodsuckers had scurried out to feast as soon as they had left. As soon as they had fled, Tommy amended.

There was a shadow overhead and Tommy glanced up fearfully. A single pink cumulous cloud was making lazy progress across the clear sky.

Don't let the nerves get to you!

22

The sun was touching the horizon when they came to a large, rusted door. A sign there read:

Private property: All trespassers will be prosecuted to the full extent of the law.

Buck was the first to laugh, followed by Tommy, before Tig and Allan joined in. Buck tossed each of them a miner's hat. Predictably, Tig's made him look like a twelve-year-old. Nerves were raw for sure, because all four of them were bent over cackling for nearly a full minute.

Laughter was the best damn therapy on Earth, Tommy thought as he gathered himself, stepped forward and slammed the heel of his boot into the door. The door swung wide and the sound of weakened metal giving way echoed back at them from inside.

Buck held his shotgun cradled over one arm. "It's now or never, gentlemen," he said and vanished into the dusty darkness.

The dark narrow corridor opened onto an enormous factory floor. The size of it made Tommy think he'd been sucked into one of those dusty old photographs; Grand Central Station during the twenties, dotted with figures long dead, rushing off to nowhere.

Streamers of vertical light bled in from above. A cathedral of steel and broken glass. The blast furnace and most of the billet casters were gone—sold or plundered over thirty years ago, when Keisel's was shut down. A few hulking remnants remained, standing guard in the murkiness like titans.

They're watching us, these machines, Tommy thought.

When he found himself cutting a wide swath to avoid a slab caster with a face full of sharp edges, he pushed the thought from his mind.

23

In the distance, a single ladder led up and into darkness.

Buck stopped and motioned toward it, his face set. "That's where we're headed."

"How do you know?" Tig asked him.

Buck turned back just long enough to catch his eye. There wasn't a touch of humor in Buck's face anymore. "It's up there. In the dark. Waiting. I can feel it."

Tig grew quiet, his eyes tracing the ladder's dim edges.

Allan stopped and propped his hands on his knees, in a half-sitting position.

"You all right, big fella?" Tommy asked him.

Allan nodded, but there was nothing convincing about it.

"I'll go first," Tommy offered. Pain was flaring in his shoulder again and blood trickled out in long red fingers from under his bandage. But it wasn't the pain that worried Tommy, so much as the blood.

They stood at the foot of the ladder. Buck shifted the weight of the heavy bag and listened. A thin scratching noise, like the skittering of tiny feet, drifted down from the darkness above.

"Rats," Buck offered. Each of them took a moment to digest the explanation. One by one they nodded their agreement, knowing full well the chances were better than none that not a single rat was left within a mile of the place.

They were maybe halfway up the ladder, Allan huffing like he was on the last leg of the Boston marathon, when the metal rung supporting Tommy gave way. It was rusted and weak, like almost everything in the dump, and perhaps, in his growing eagerness to escape the vulnerable position they now found themselves in, Tommy had yanked a little too hard. The sound of snapping metal rang sharply in his ears. He screamed and

24

scrambled for purchase. Rusted flakes of metal stabbed his hands as he slid directly into Allan, whose weight saved Tommy from falling to his death. The twisted rung spiralled past them in slow motion, heading for a large metal drum below. Buck snapped his hand out to grab it, and for a moment, his fingers actually touched it, or at least he thought they did, but the bar skittered away from him.

The ear crushing racket the rung made when it hit the metal drum made Tommy cringe. It sounded to Tommy like the gong used to summon King Kong in the old black and white movie. The men remained still, Tommy panting, praying, but more importantly, listening for the scratching.

They all listened.

The scratching was gone.

Then the swooping came. Whoomp, Whoomp, Whoomp. Tig and Allan searched in vain through the darkness. "Sounds so big," Tig said and his voice sounded panicky. Bringing up the rear, he had reason to be worried.

"Everyone to the top! Fast!" Buck shouted.

The men began scrambling, their arms and legs pistoning up and down, as if powering a V8 engine.

A huge gust of foul wind swept past them and the force of it sent the hair on Tommy's head whipping into his eyes. They were so terribly vulnerable right now ...

Stay cool, Tommy told himself.

He grabbed for the next rung and saw himself miss it. Saw himself falling backwards, his arms flailing. The world turned upside down. He felt the wind in his hair, cool against the back of his neck, slick with sweat, and everything was quiet. He wanted to look back and see what he was falling into, but a part of him was resigned to his fate.

Snap out of it! There are worse things than falling, he told himself. *Like being plucked up and carried away.*

And if that happened there would be no snapping of claws this time, not this high up. A blur of movement registered in the corner of his eye. He turned his head enough to see the creature swooping down on them from the shadows, its wings splayed wide, like a hawk going for a squirrel. It shrieked and Tommy wanted so badly to cover his ears. Instead he reached into the band of his jeans and pulled out the .45. Inside the building, the beast was little more than a blur, but it was a big blur and he aimed for the middle of it and squeezed off a round.

Nothing.

He fired again. And again. It was twenty feet away now, and closing in fast. The guys below were shouting for him to move. He shoved the gun under his belt and raced for the landing that could surely not be much further. He hoped their movement might make them a difficult target. In part, Tommy was right; it did help.

There was another rush of air and this time, Tommy was nudged by the leathery membrane of a wing. From below, Buck shouted. The beast had tried to grab him and missed, knocking the blue duffel bag from Buck's hands in the process. Tig's wiry arm shot out and caught hold of it. The bag was heavy and the weight of it nearly peeled the skinny man off the ladder. Tig steadied himself and then swung it over his shoulder. Buck was about to congratulate his friend, when Tig began to scream. The monster was back and the claws on its feet had curled around Tig's rib cage. Tig was trying to reach for the Winchester, slung across his back, but the blue bag was in the way. The creature was pulling at him with its taloned feet.

A kind of sick tug of war was going on between this thing and the ladder. Before he could reach out to help him, Tommy heard Tig's fingers give way and for a

26

moment, man and creature were free falling through the air before a final snatch and a thrust from the creature's powerful wings carried him off. In spite of his friend's screams, and the unbelievable pain, Tommy witnessed the unbelievable; Tig's hand reached behind him, his index finger searching for the Winchester's trigger hole. He found it at last and his hand jerked. The gun kicked back and a spray of blood and bone exploded from the back of his head and the creature's abdomen. The creature screamed its horrible woman's scream and let Tig go. His limp body spiraled lifelessly through the air, before it smashed into the ground with a muffled thump.

The three remaining men stared into the darkness below for what felt like an eternity. Then the beast circled back.

Not far above him, Tommy swore he could see a hatch. He was climbing again, with renewed enthusiasm. He reached it so quickly that he bumped the top of his head. His hand pressed against the trap door and a current of cool air tickled his palm. Thin lines of light revealed where the edges were. He gave it a push and as he did, he heard Buck's voice: "It's coming back, Tommy. Hurry!"

But the door wouldn't budge. Then he saw the lock, smiling back at him gleefully.

"Motherfucker!"

"Tommy!" It was Buck again and this time Allan had joined him.

Tommy pulled the .45 out and turned away. "Watch out," he called to them before he fired at the lock. The creature shrieked. When he looked back, the lock was shattered. He shoved the door open and pulled himself up onto the landing. Hunched over the hole, he reached down and grasped Allan by the back of his pants and heaved the fat man up. Buck was last and no sooner did Tommy have him in hand than the creature crashed into the ladder. The entire room shuddered. The creature folded its wings and as Tommy pulled Buck through the gap, it ambled up the ladder after them.

Buck and Allan collapsed in exhaustion.

"Close the hatch!" Tommy screamed at them.

The beast's flattened head was already halfway into the room when they sprung to their feet. Its glowing red eyes skittered across the room and seized on Buck. Buck swung the hatch with every ounce of strength he had. Tommy pulled out his .45. Allan stood immobilized, his Springfield prone at his feet.

The hatch buckled as it hit the creature in the head and then slammed shut, silencing the animal's cry. There was a pile of cinderblocks in the corner and Tommy brought one over and placed it on the hatch cover.

"Pile them up so he can't get through," Buck said.

"We coulda had him," Tommy said, heaving another cinderblock. "One shot to the temple and he woulda been a dog's dinner."

Allan's face looked like a wet rag. He staggered toward the trap door and the pile of cinderblocks. "We gotta see if Tig's alri—"

Buck blocked his way. "Were you napping back there? Tig's deader than President Grant. Killed himself so he wouldn't be taken ali—"

Allan's face was bright red. "Tig isn't dead." Spittle flew from his lips. "What about all those people who can't open their parachutes and live? It happens."

Buck's eyes didn't waver. Both men stood toe to toe, glaring at one another. "I know what I saw, Allan, and no amount of your denial's gonna change that."

Tommy slid in between them. "Allan, I know you and Tig go way back. I know you loved him like a brother. But Tig's dead. You saw it yourself. No amount of risking our skin down there's gonna bring him back." He pointed over to Allan's Springfield, lying against a rotted mattress. "Now pick up your gun."

Allan's eyes fell to the hatch and wouldn't budge. Tommy slapped the man's fleshy cheek. Allan's eyes flashed with anger. "Snap out of it, will ya?" Tommy shouted. "We need you, right now. What happened to Tig was bad, but we gotta put the bad behind us and do what it is we came here to do."

Tommy caught sight of Buck and couldn't immediately place the expression on the old man's face. It was an expression that worried him. Before long, he recognized the shadow he saw forming behind his friend's eyes for what it was: obsession.

Tommy crossed to the old mattress and fell onto it, sending a cloud of dust into the air. He removed his .45 and reached into his pants pocket for more bullets. Allan sunk to the ground, his eyes frantically scanning the room, his lips quivering, ever so slightly.

The room they now found themselves in looked like a foreman's office. In the corner, there were the remnants of an old desk, now no more than an overturned heap of crumpled wood. Buck approached an old water cooler and flipped the lever back and forth a few times, to no avail. Tommy was loading bullets into the Colt's magazine when a noise shattered his concentration. The scratching was back, this time louder. Like a thousand tiny feet scuttling about.

"Mommy's home," Buck chimed in and at once, all three men had a nearly identical thought.

She's brought dinner.

But none of them had the nerve to undo their barricade of cinder blocks and check to see if Tig's body was still lying on the dusty patch of ground at the bottom of the ladder, though each of them was more than positive that it wasn't.

For Buck, it was the loss of the dynamite that was his gravest concern. He moved to the doorway, shotgun in hand. "All right, let's go."

Tommy took point. Buck followed up to the rear. They headed down a narrow hallway; closed doors lined either side, making them wonder what horrors were lurking on the other side. The air was dusty, swirling into shadow as the men passed. They were searching for the source of the scratching; at least that was the unspoken understanding.

"Find what's making that noise," Buck said, "and you find what needs to be killed."

Part IV
'End Game'

The mining helmets cast three long, ghostly beams before them, swords of light stabbing into the lurking shadows. Buck pointed to a door on their left. They approached it, Allan now behind the other two men. Tommy bent forward and pressed his ear flat against the door.

The room sounded empty.

Tommy turned the knob slowly and then threw the door open. Yellow light cut through the shadows, revealing more ruined desks, two old typewriters, a chalkboard, but not much else.

There was a disappointed look on Buck's face, like he'd expected to find something more. Something else.

"Uh, guys," Allan whispered from the hallway. "Guys?"

"What is it, Allan?" Buck retorted in the reproachful tone usually reserved for children who are wearing thin on the nerves.

"Should there be a breeze in here?"

Buck and Tommy exchanged a puzzled glance.

"You two better get out here."

They did, and were met by one of Allan's chubby fingers pointing down the hallway. Their eyes followed it. The beams from their helmets crawled along the corridor,

31

illuminating a door, some thirty feet away, swaying lazily on its hinges, back and forth, as though a gentle breeze were nudging it.

One of the few remaining scraps of Buck's hair kept the same beat.

Buck approached it at a brisk pace, Tommy in tow. When the latter turned back, he saw that Allan was still rooted in place, looking like a bronzed version of the Hamburgler.

"Allan! Front and center," Tommy hissed.

Allan didn't move.

"You stay behind, one of those things is gonna grind you up for mush and use you as baby food."

For a moment, Allan's eyes lost that glazed, stupid look.

"For Tig," Tommy said finally. "We don't set this right then he died for nothing."

Allan's lips were pursed. He nodded and swung the butt of his Springfield up and caught the business end with his free hand.

"For Tig," he said.

"Yes, for Tig," Tommy whispered, "and everyone else these things will get, unless …"

When Tommy turned back, Buck was gone. He hurried to the swaying door and pulled it open. Inside was Buck, looking more than a little frustrated. Despite its perceived promise, the room seemed to hold nothing new. Buck and Allan stooped down to investigate a bundle of clothing; bloodied jeans and t-shirts were tossed haphazardly on the floor. Just then, something cold slid down and brushed against Tommy's left cheek. Tommy brought his fingers to his cheek and then held them under the yellow light of his helmet. The substance was thick and slimy.

Tommy's eyes ran up the wall toward the ceiling and what he saw there sucked all the breath out of his body.

A hole in the ceiling, maybe five feet in diameter; not enormous, but wide enough for the biggest of those things to squeeze through. The edges were soft and worn, giving him the uncomfortable illusion that he was standing underneath some great, black bowel. For a second, Tommy managed to tear his eyes away and saw that Buck and Allan had seen it too. This would be their way in. Only problem was, it was a healthy ten feet from the floor to the ceiling.

Tommy dragged a sagging desk over and centered it underneath the hole.

"If we pile up enough of this crap, we may be able to crawl through—"

Allan's face bore the expression of a man who'd spent the last twenty minutes in the spin cycle.

"No goddamn way am I going up there! Ain't no way!"

Tommy was dragging an old filing cabinet toward the center of the room. When the pile was over five feet high, he grabbed hold of a desk leg and attempted to scramble up.

"Gimme a hand, will ya?" Tommy asked Buck as his legs wobbled, feeling like a child learning to walk for the first time.

Buck placed a hand on Tommy's back to stabilize him, looking doubtful "This ain't gonna hold us. Specially not Allan with all that extra baggage he's carrying."

"I-I juh-just told you," Allan stammered. "I'm not going up there."

Tommy teetered at the top of the pile and stretched a hand up, his heart pounding in his chest. He had seen what those things could do to a man's face.

There was a sudden moan as the pile beneath him began to shift. Tommy struggled to keep his balance. Just then his foot tore through a section of rotten wood planking, swallowing his leg to the knee. Tommy bit

33

down on his lip as pain stung him. A thick splinter of wood bit into his calf, tearing through his pant leg.

Buck jumped up and yanked him free. A trail of blood followed them. All three men stared at the wound, the trickle of viscous blood, and then back at the hole in the ceiling. Bleak faced. Fearful.

"This is not good," Buck said gravely.

"Tie it off quickly," Allan pleaded, "before they start coming."

Buck caught Allan's eyes. "Go get some of those cinder blocks. We'll pile 'em. It's the only way we'll get up there."

Allan nodded, just happy to have an excuse to get away from the hole in the ceiling. Buck tied off Tommy's wound and helped him to his feet.

"I really fucked up this time, didn't I, Buck?"

"You've done plenty worse," he said with a tight smile.

"Ah, thanks."

"How's the leg?"

Tommy stood, wavered for a moment and then hobbled around the room, moving with the grace of a man with a rock in his shoe.

"I'll be fine, really. Don't worry about me." Despite his bravado, Tommy *was* worried. Not about himself; mostly about the thing that had been bothering him since he'd first seen Buck's mangled hand: the blood. Tommy could feel it saturating his pant leg and knew it was the silent equivalent of ringing a dinner bell. Buck knew it too, but neither man said a word. They did the only thing they could under the circumstances. They helped Allan move cinderblocks.

● ● ●

That the walls of the narrow passageway were slick and syrupy didn't bother Tommy all that much. Crawling through the goo that had collected on the floor, however, did. He could feel the strange substance oozing into the open wounds on his shoulder and he wondered what medical problems he would discover if he ever made it out of there alive. Allan had refused to follow them inside, perhaps because the idea of getting stuck in a hole like a pig in a blanket frightened him more than the prospect of taking his chances alone. The beams from their helmets cut through the darkness. Not far ahead they could see that the tunnel opened into a larger chamber.

Where we might finally be able to stand up, Tommy thought hopefully.

Tommy was in front of Buck and when he came to the mouth of the larger room, he froze.

"What's wrong?" Buck snarled from the rear.

Tommy slid forward on his elbows. As the two men stood, their jaws slackened, their breathing became ragged and desperate, like two fish plucked from a half-gallon bowl. To Tommy, the room looked like it might once have been a cafeteria or an assembly hall. Now it looked like a morgue. Laid out neatly around them were dozens of bodies. Men, women, and children alike. But morgue wasn't exactly the right word, since these people were still alive. At least, they seemed alive. Their bodies wriggled and twitched, ever so slightly.

No, they weren't wriggling, Tommy realized.

Beneath their clothing, their skin rippled like waves at the beach on a blustery day. Except these waves were unique; they were slow and purposeful. There was something else about the bodies that struck Tommy as odd. They were all obese. Buck and Tommy approached a bloated man with blond curly hair. His eyes were closed, his enormous belly ebbing and flowing. Buck bent down and slid a hand beneath the man's head.

"Buddy, wake up! We're gonna take you outta here!"

The wriggling stopped. Then the man's mouth opened. He was about to speak. Buck moved closer to hear. Now the man's face began to distort and stretch. His mouth gaped open so wide his lips were splitting apart.

Tommy grabbed Buck to pull him away, but it was too late. A fleshy appendage sprang from the man's broken face and latched onto Buck's neck. Blood spurted in a straight and powerful arc and Buck screamed, his arms thrashing about. Tommy fumbled for his gun, dropping it in his haste onto the man's deflated torso. Buck grabbed the creature with his bare hands and squeezed. The tips of his fingers, followed by the length of his digits in their entirety, disappeared into the creature's pink, blood spattered flesh. Thick, white puss began to run down Buck's arms, as he struggled with what looked like a fat worm, with needles for teeth. At last, Tommy got a handle on his Colt, and brought it to the creature's head, not two inches from Buck's lower jaw and pulled the trigger. Buck's face was splashed with more of the creature's bone white blood. The worm collapsed to the floor and lay still. Buck held a hand up to his neck. Blood trickled between his fingers. Tommy ripped the left sleeve off his shirt and tied it around Buck's neck.

"What in hell was that?" Tommy cried. "What is this place?"

Buck scanned the room. He was thinking about his neck and wondering how long it would take the rest of them to smell the blood. "Looks like we found the nursery," he said finally. And as he spoke, Tommy noticed that the flowing movement along the floor had ceased. The bodies had grown still and for a second, he thought that they almost looked human again. Almost. Within a moment, all around, mouths were opening. Dozens of mouths, opening and releasing their prizes, like the fat man with the big belly and the curly blond hair.

"Run!" Buck shouted.

There was a hallway up ahead, maybe twenty paces away. They bolted, weaving between the deflating bodies. From Buck's right, a larva with a mouthful of needle-sharp teeth sprang from its host toward them. Buck leveled his shotgun and pulled the trigger. There was an echoing boom. The shotgun gave a mighty kick and the worm's head disintegrated before them. Its body flopped to the ground, convulsing.

"Wait," Tommy shouted.

Buck skidded to a stop and turned.

Tommy was beckoning him over. "It's Tig!"

Tig's shattered body looked like someone had broken it on the rack. His right leg sat at a queer ninety degree angle, and his neck was cocked so far to one side it had to be broken. Buck reached down, grabbed the blue duffel bag from Tig's mangled shoulder and shouted. "Let's go!"

"We can't just leave him! Those things …"

Buck caught sight of movement behind Tommy.

"Get down!" Buck screamed. Instinctively, Tommy dropped to the floor. There was a deafening bang and a warm spray on Tommy's face.

"This whole place'll just be a memory in another ten minutes," Buck said coldly. "We can't take him with us. Now come on!"

Tommy was limping badly. In front of him, Buck, wheezing hard, was blasting a path for them with his shotgun.

The hallway was narrow, ending in a flight of stairs. Behind them larvae were pouring into the corridor.

"These things don't give up, do they?" Tommy said. "Let's just set the dynamite and get out of here."

Buck's eyes were scanning the hallway and the approaching worms. "We have to be sure."

"Sure … sure of what?"

"That big bitch, she's what we're after. I'm certain of it. Maybe I made a mistake coming here in the first place, setting all this off. Or maybe it was gonna happen anyway. Regardless, if we blow this place then we gotta be sure she goes with it."

Tommy's heart sank. The idea made the pain in his shoulder scream out with blinding agony. It wasn't so long ago that *that thing* had sent him careening through the air and he wasn't in any hurry to repeat the maneuver.

The larvae were still coming. Squirming mindlessly over one another, the single-minded, pulsating instinct to feed driving them forward.

"We better hope we're heading in the right direction," Tommy said. He turned to Buck, but Buck was already gone.

When Tommy caught up to him, Buck had ascended the staircase and was starting down an impossibly long hallway.

As they made their way along, the only sound was the muffled, rhythmic clunk of their heavy boots on the concrete floor. Clunk clunk, clunk clunk. "Those things were eating those people …" Tommy trailed off. He was shaking his head, trying to find the words to express his incredulity.

"Blowflies," Buck answered enigmatically.

"Eh?"

"Blowflies spend their lives looking for dead things to lay their eggs in." He was reloading his shotgun, counting the number of shells he had left, trying not to look worried. "When the eggs hatch, the larvae eat the body

38

from the inside until they're old enough to get food on their own."

Tommy let out a dry, nervous laugh. "I doubt those things have any trouble getting food on their own."

Clunk clunk, clunk clunk, scrape.

Tommy was about to say something else when he heard the sound of tiny claws scurrying about. He regulated his breathing, straining to listen. No, it didn't sound like it was above them *this* time. Ahead of them was an old rusted metal door. *Could they be on the other side of it?* he wondered anxiously. *Or are they behind us?* He felt icy fingers of fear crawling up his spine but shook the feeling away.

"Stop for a moment, will ya?" Tommy called out.

Buck stopped.

"You hear that?"

Buck seemed to concentrate, then shook his head.

And he was right. The noise wasn't there anymore. Was he cracking up? After watching that grotesque worm, dripping with some guy's innards latch onto Buck's neck, anything was possible. Buck was walking away now. Tommy sped after him, a quickness in his staggered step.

Clunk clunk, clunk clunk.

Scrape scrape.

Tommy's headlamp began to dim just as the noise came back, before flickering and dying completely. The scratching was getting louder, he realized, and the nature of the sound was also changing. It sounded dull, almost like claws scuttling along the ground. No, not almost, it sounded exactly like scrapping claws. Tommy spun around and saw blackness. He smacked the side of his helmet. The light flicked back to life momentarily and then died again, but in that instant, he had seen nearly enough to turn every hair on his head milky white. Not ten yards behind them, dozens of red glowing eyes were staring back at him, their bird-like bodies ambling stealthily down the hallway. The last thing Tommy saw before his light dimmed and faded forever was the creatures breaking into a mad dash, clawing at the walls to get at them.

"Oh my God, they're right behind us, Buck!"

Buck turned to look at Tommy and his eyes became saucers.

"Move your ass!" Tommy shouted, staggering past him, bad leg and all.

They were screaming now, those things behind them. They were getting closer and they could smell the blood. Maybe even taste it.

Buck's light bobbed and cast a sick shadow against the door at the end of the hall. *If it's locked*, Tommy thought, *we're doomed*. There were too many of them to kill. Not enough time to reload. Frantic with terror, Tommy promised himself he would keep a single bullet, just in case.

They came to the metal door and to Tommy's mounting horror, he saw Buck enable to open it. The old man rattled the handle back and forth, but to no avail. The knob had no key hole, so how could it be locked? Tommy wanted to scream.

"Get down," Buck shouted as he spun on his heels, leveled his shotgun and almost deafened Tommy with the concussion from its blast. There was an explosion of fur and blood. Two creatures fell and were promptly stampeded by those that came from behind them.

"Jeeeesus," Buck whispered. "Didn't even slow 'em down. Ten more seconds before those things make chicken feed out of us, Tommy. Do something!"

Tommy crawled passed him and scanned the doorframe anxiously and that's when he saw it: a thick metal slide-latch protruding from the overhead arch. He yanked it down, the muscles in his great forearms bulging as they contracted. His injured shoulder burned with the effort of it. At first, nothing happened; then came the glorious sound of screeching metal as the latch—no doubt older than either of them—broke free. Tommy turned the knob, kicked the door with his good foot and disappeared inside, Buck tight on his heels. They slammed the door shut together and not a second later, felt it shudder under the weight of the creatures on the other side. Tommy could hear their nails scraping in the darkness, but otherwise they were quiet. Perhaps those things knew something they didn't. Tommy and Buck remained with their backs braced against the door. Barely a moment later, the sounds from the hallway was gone.

Buck raked the area with the meagre light from his helmet. They were in an enormous cathedral-like chamber. In the distance, they could hear dripping water. The damp smell of ammonia was almost overpowering, making their nostrils burn.

"You think they left?" Tommy whispered.

Buck gave him a look. "You feel like takin' a peek?" he whispered back.

Tommy shook his head and was tempted to tell Buck to go fuck himself. He was quiet for a moment, almost pensive. "Why are we whispering?"

"I'm not sure."

Tommy's nerves almost made him explode into laughter but he held it inside.

"We got to find something to prop against this door," Buck told him.

There was an old dusty vending machine near a pile of broken furniture. Tommy stuck a hand underneath it and began dragging it over. The sound of screeching metal was awful. Tommy was breathing hard, rocking it back and forth. When he arrived, Buck helped him move it into place.

41

"There," Buck said finally, brushing rusty particles off his hands and admiring their work. "That should hold 'em."

Tommy couldn't hide the concern on his face.

"What's wrong?"

"You think Allan's all right?"

"That fat ol' bastard?" Buck said, trying to sound hard, but realizing his own unease was probably showing. "I'm sure he's fine."

Just then, something soft landed on Tommy's head and slide down his face. It almost felt like a clump of warm mud. Buck saw it and doubled over. The stench of it made Tommy gag. He scrapped it off his face with a cupped hand. The floor was wet with puddled water and he went to clean himself. But the minute he brought his cupped hand to his face he knew something was terribly wrong. This puddle on the floor wasn't water. And that stuff hadn't been mud.

He looked up at Buck. Buck was leaning on the vending machine, fighting off insane spasms of laughter, his great barrel chest heaving up and down.

"Buck," Tommy said faintly, pointing toward the ceiling.

That made Buck laugh all the more, tears were rolling down his cheeks. It was almost a full minute before Buck regained his composure. That there wasn't an ounce of humor in Tommy's eyes had helped. Slowly, ever so slowly, Buck traced the light from his helmet up the edge of the wall and onto the high gambrel ceiling. The ceiling was sloped—both men beginning to feel as though they were standing inside the biggest barn on earth. The beam from Buck's helmet dissipated to a faint glow as it reached the ceiling. Something up there in the shadows was moving. Lots of somethings.

Then Tommy saw what was there, what the movement belonged to, he was sure his eyes had to be playing tricks on him. He looked at Buck and whatever hope he had of being delusional evaporated like a patch of water on the ground in the Sahara. The old man's face visibly blanched.

Above them, negotiating the ceiling with sublime ease, were what had to be a hundred creatures, their wings fluttering now and again, some of them scrambling over one another, angling for a better place. They seemed to be in some kind of rest cycle, but even so, the ceiling was filled with so much movement it hardly seemed believable. A cold fear was coursing through Tommy as he remembered wrestling that vending machine. The way it squeaked and groaned. He felt vulnerable. His gut tightened with the thought of how close he had come to waking a hundred eating machines.

"She's up there," Buck whispered. There was good reason to whisper now. "You see'er?"

Tommy strained, fighting the gnawing urge to run.

"The big one near the middle." Buck motioned with his hand and that's when Tommy saw her, near the center of the great insectile mass.

"Look at 'er, sitting there, cool as a cucumber while the others scurry around her."

"Her children," Tommy said.

Buck's eyes met his. "That's right."

The strange, obsessive quality in Buck's eyes ignited something deep within Tommy's memory. Years ago, in junior high, he had read a story—the very remembrance of which felt so distant from this moment, that it might as well have been another life. Distant or not, the rough edges of the tale had come back to him with shocking suddenness. It was the story of how a man's obsession with killing a mythical white whale had proven to be his undoing. It had become something personal for the guy in the book, a sort of payback, and it was that same kind

43

of obsession that Tommy could see on Buck's face now. The dangerous look of a man coming unhinged.

They were bound, somehow, these two. Buck and this beast.

Buck extended an arm and let the handles of the blue duffel bag slide down into the palm of his hand. He pulled the zipper, reached inside and removed ten sticks of dynamite. They were lashed together with duct tape, and in the center was a small round-faced clock, multi-colored wires pouring out of it.

Tommy eyed the contraption with reverence.

"We got ourselves a problem," Buck said quietly.

"Problem?" Tommy whispered.

Buck pointed with the dim light from his helmet. "Y'see that port hole up there?"

Up close to where the two halves of the roof met was a dark hole, a nook. The kind of place where a bird might set up a nest.

"What of it?" Tommy asked.

"That must be how they're coming and going."

"So?"

"So if we set these sticks too low, we might not get 'em all, especially if some of 'em manage to escape onto the roof."

"So what are you saying?" Tommy questioned, although he thought he knew perfectly well what Buck was saying. Over by a peeling worker safety board, was the mouth of what appeared to be an old service elevator. "Buck, I don't know about this. That thing hasn't been powered in years."

Buck's eyes were dim. "I'm not taking any elevator ride, Tommy," he said. "Shafts like these always have a ladder inside 'em. May even connect with that hole they made. I'll set the timer for ten minutes, that should be enough. Then I'll slam dunk 'em with it!" Buck's face lit up. "Assuming that ladder ain't busted, I should back within six minutes." His gaze met Tommy's. "If I don't return in five, you start outta here like it ain't nobody's business."

"Buck, let me go, I can be back sooner."

Buck waved him away. "With that bum leg of yours? I started this and you can bet your ass I'm gonna finish it. Those things are gonna wish they'd kept hibernatin' another hundred years."

Buck grabbed Tommy's shoulders and pulled him close, squeezing him. Before Tommy could say another word, Buck had let go, slung the shotgun and the blue duffel bag over his shoulder and was gone.

Buck's headlamp bobbed and gradually faded in the distance before Tommy grasped what was really happening. The weight of it hit him so hard that for a moment he felt the breath seize in his lungs. The old man hadn't gone off to face them alone; he'd gone off to die. The six minutes there and back had been a bluff. He had no intention of returning. He was going to climb that ladder, plant the explosives and open up on the 'queen bee' in a hail of gore and glory. He was gonna take her with him. Tommy started toward the elevator. Toward the sound of flapping wings overhead. No way was he going to let the old man off that easy.

When he came to the elevator, the doors were open, but the hatch that led into the shaft and was locked.

Damnit! Tommy thought. *The old bastard knew I'd come after him.*

He remembered reading an article in Maxim magazine about escaping from stuck elevators and how some of them had side doors for that very purpose. Tommy pulled his Zippo from his pocket, flipped the lid and struck it against his jeans. The walls of the car wavered in an orange glow. He was looking for a vertical edge or at least a hinge of some sort and he was so concentrated on the task he didn't hear the flapping of wings or the sound of clawed hands landing in the shallow puddles outside.

"There we go," Tommy said triumphantly as his hand slipped beneath the wood paneling and hit upon what felt like a steel handle. It was at approximately the same time that his nose wrinkled at the pungent odor of rotting flesh. Accompanying that odor was the overwhelming sensation he was being watched. He turned quickly, stabbing a hand into the seat of his pants for his Colt. He was going to swing the gun out and lay waste to whatever it was that had come sneaking up behind him. He was quick, very quick, but the beast was quicker. It was young, just old enough to fly perhaps, its skin pallid and wormlike. Still too young to have any real sense of caution, it lunged through the open elevator doors with incredible speed, knocking both gun and lighter to the floor. Standing face to face, it grasped Tommy's ankles with its powerful lower claws and held his arms with its stubby upper limbs. The beast was trying to wrestle him to the ground, pin him down where gravity would push its gnashing jaws onto his face. He outweighed it, but the muscles in the creature's body were compact and powerful. It was a fine specimen, and he might have found room to admire it, were it not trying to rip his face off. Then it did something amazing; the edge of its wings reached out and seized the walls of the elevator car: it was trying to stabilize itself in an effort to force Tommy to the ground. For the first time Tommy felt a hot stinging panic. It would soon be on top of him, and then it would feed. Its fangs sinking into the soft flesh under his chin, coming away greedily with the delicious fruit that was his Adam's apple. It would all be over soon. Outside he could hear another set of leathery wings folding in place and a set of clawed feet splashing down. They were starting to land.

What took you sonsabitches so long? he thought sickly.

The flame from his lighter was dancing off the barrel of his Colt not two feet from his arm. He was in a supine position now, the creature lashing out at him desperately with a mouth full of needle-sharp teeth. Tommy knew he stood no chance, lying prone and pinned as he was. The second creature was approaching now, curious. In desperation, Tommy began rocking the animal from side to side, shifting his weight in an effort to unbalance it. He could see his own fearful face reflected in the bulge of its great insectile eyes. Then he gave a final thrust and sent it crashing to the ground. The creature braced itself using the edge of its wing. Its mouth opened to swallow his face, but all it found was the barrel of his .45. Three muffled shots rang out and the bird-creature slumped to the ground, its eyes staring at nothing.

Two more creatures landed just outside the elevator.

Another was ambling through the elevator doors. It was looking at the body lying atop of Tommy. Its expression changed. There was confusion in its wretched face, then understanding, then something like anger. Its eyes locked onto Tommy's and he pulled the trigger. The large .45 caliber round entered in through the creature's right eye and tore half its face away. The animal fell to its knees and then tumbled forward. Tommy kicked the body of the first creature off of him and scrambled to get up.

Three shots left, he thought wildly. *Three shots left before I have to reload.*

Outside there were at least six creatures on the ground and who knew how many more flying above them. They had heard the shots, no doubt. *.45's just a bit louder'an a squeaky old vending machine.*

The next creature was older than the others. Its graying fur was mottled and even. Tommy was standing now, Zippo in one hand, Colt in the other. Its saucer-plate eyes were locked hypnotically on Tommy.

Tommy's first two shots hit the creature in the chest. It stumbled back, its movements eerily human-like, then it caught the edge of the elevator doors with its wings and kept coming. Tommy dropped it with his last bullet. He had more. He'd brought over twenty in all, but there wasn't time to reload. He had to get out of there. Any thoughts of making a run for it were dashed, however, when two more of the creatures touched down and began ambling toward the elevator doors. Tommy held up his gun, as if to scare them off, but they didn't even flinch. He might as well have been holding up a cheeseburger. They kept coming, in single file.

The lower jaw of the first fell open and out spilled a resoundingly shrill cry. Tommy reached into his pocket and fingered three bullets out. His fingers were shaking something awful and the bullets spilled to the ground. The creatures sank on their haunches, ready to spring. The room exploded with an ear shattering boom. Both creatures' heads came apart like ripe melons, dropped from a ten story building. Tommy looked up to find Buck climbing down from the open hatch.

"I leave you alone for five minutes and you nearly get yourself killed." Buck looked genuinely angry.

Tommy saw that Buck still had the blue duffel bag. Buck followed Tommy's gaze. "Course I didn't have time. Barely got my arse up halfway when I heard a whole Fourth of July going off down here."

The two men hustled out and into the open. They were heading toward the vending machine and the bolted door. Above them, the ceiling was swirling as though some great gray waltz were in full swing.

Buck slowed and then skidded to a stop. "She's up there, Tommy, I can see her."

48

"Forget about her," Tommy said desperately. "We gotta get outta here, there are too many of them!"

Tommy grabbed Buck by the arm and tore him away. When they arrived at the barricaded door, Tommy began pulling at the vending machine. Buck's attention was still fixated above them. The mass was descending. They would be landing soon, the lot of them.

Buck removed the stack of dynamite and fingered the timer switch. "Fifteen minutes should be enough, no?"

Tommy looked back in horror. "What? Buck, you're not setting that thing! We don't even know what's on the other side of this door!"

"You're right," he said. "Better make it ten."

A dozen or so birdmen were splashing down by the elevator. Tommy tugged at the door, the vending machine skidding a few inches further away from it with every pull. He glanced over his shoulder.

The room was dim as Buck—with the only light between them—was using it to set the dynamite. Each time Buck glanced up, Tommy could see the creatures getting closer, their red, soulless eyes gleaming.

There were so many of them, Tommy thought. A few were still circling overhead.

The old man held the shotgun in the crook of his arm and Tommy took it from him now. He leveled it and fired. A few of them staggered back, one or two fluttered into the air and then landed again, but on they came, faster now, as though they could sense the fear in the air. Or the blood.

"They're still too far to set this thing off," Buck said without looking up. He put his ear to the clock on the dynamite, listening for a tick. It was working.

They bundled it back in the bag and slid the package atop the vending machine. The creatures were nearly on them now.

Tommy took Buck's helmet from him, strapped it on and squeezed through the narrow opening into the long hallway. Buck was right behind him.

Tommy was about to close the door when Buck spotted 'Mama' touching down not ten feet from the vending machine.

"Give me the gun!" Buck shouted. Maybe it was the light playing tricks, but for the first time Tommy could see dark rings around Buck's eyes.

"We don't have time, Buck, close the door!"

"Tommy!"

"We don't—"

Buck snatched the shotgun out of Tommy's hands and tried pushing his way back into the room. Tommy grabbed him around the waist, pulling with everything he had. The gun went off and fired wide. Tommy clenched his teeth, stuck a foot against the door frame and leaned into it, flinging himself and the old man backwards. There was the sound of tearing metal and glass as the vending machine was swept aside and in that moment, all Tommy could think about was the dynamite.

Don't let it detonate early. Oh please.

Then he thought about the door. If they couldn't close it in time, they would be overrun. Tommy scrambled to his feet and leapt for the door handle. As he grabbed it, a large clawed hand appeared through the opening and closed around his arm. A sharp stab of vicious pain tore through the left side of his body.

"Move!" Buck shouted.

Tommy dropped and Buck aimed the barrel of his shotgun at the creature's arm and fired, point blank. There was a terrible scream. Blood, the color of old milk, painted the door and the faces of both men. The mutilated arm retracted, but the clawed hand remained, blood still pumping out in mucousy white jets. Tommy shook it off and it fell with a wet plop onto the concrete

50

floor. Tommy snapped the door closed and bolted it shut. He looked at Buck and found his friend's eyes filled with bloodlust.

The silence between them was broken by a shattering boom. The door shuddered. The creatures were battering the door, trying to get in and it wouldn't be long before they succeeded.

Buck looked up from his wrist watch. "Less than eight minutes," he said matter of factly. Tommy straightened, swallowing hard. The two men began running down the long hallway, the sound of clawed hands scratching and hammering behind them.

Detonation: 7 minutes 5 seconds

When they arrived at the nursery, it was empty. The bodies were still there of course, but every single last one of them was completely deflated. If Tommy had seen a Looney Tunes steam roller tearing around, flattening everyone into a pancake, it wouldn't have surprised his beleaguered brain one bit at that point. But the emptiness wasn't a good sign, Tommy realized dully. The worms had gone somewhere and they sure as hell didn't slither up the stairs after him and Buck. So where …

Both men looked at each other with the same realization.

"Allan!"

They ran for the narrow passage, Tommy limping in the lead. They dropped once they reached the orifice so they could crawl through the slime and the stench. Tommy realized their mistake only after it was too late; they were about to drop through the ceiling, headfirst. There was no time to inch back. Tommy let the shotgun drop through the opening to the floor. It landed with a clang and he wriggled forward until he too dropped, feeling like a giant turd being squeezed into a toilet bowl. His hands took the brunt of the punishment, smashing

51

and scrapping against the pyramid of concrete blocks they'd set up earlier. Tommy's fall finished with an awkward looking cartwheel and he landed on the floor on his ass. Buck followed and was no more elegant.

Tommy snatched up the shotgun and started for the room they had left Allan in. When Tommy arrived, the blood in his veins froze. A crude barricade of old busted furniture had been erected at the end of the hall, sealing off the room with the trapdoor. A portion of the barricade had collapsed, where it had been breached. Buck and Tommy approached cautiously, uncertain of what they might find, and yet at the same time, deathly certain of what would be waiting.

6 minutes 15 seconds

Peering over the barricade, they saw Allan. Or more accurately: what was left of him. He lay in the midst of a sea of dead larvae. A terrible last stand had obviously played out here not long ago. The floor was ankle deep in white gore. A few of the creatures looked as though they'd been shot; others had the markings of being clubbed. The stained butt of Allan's rifle evidenced that. Tommy and Buck approached the corpse of their friend. Part of his left hand was missing. Around the stump he had wrapped a strip of cloth, torn from his shirt. By the looks of things, he had beaten them off one at a time as they had tried to work their way through the barricade, but at some point there had been too many of them and he had been overwhelmed.

Tommy reached down to wipe the blood from Allan's swollen face and the fat man's eyes snapped open.

Tommy jumped back. Allan was scrambling for his gun.

"Easy, Allan, it's us!" Buck shouted.

Allan stopped fumbling. Tears welled in his eyes. His face was deathly pale, his lips beryl blue.

52

"He's lost a lot of blood," Tommy said. "Allan, can you walk?"

Allan nodded, made a strained effort to get up, and then shook his head.

"Staying here and tending to him like Florence Nightingale ain't a luxury we can afford," Buck said and scooped the fat man up and over his shoulder, rocking back on his heels as he did so.

Allan moaned in pain.

"Can we make it down that ladder with him like this?" Tommy asked.

Allan was reaching for his gun.

Buck said to Allan: "It's no good to you anymore, Allan. You can tell your ma it misfired and nearly took your hand off. Maybe she'll go easy on you. Tommy, get the bloody door, will ya?"

5 minutes 30 seconds

Blocking the trapdoor were three cinderblocks and the bodies of two larvae. Tommy kicked the corpses aside with disgust—the feeling was very much like kicking a wet pile of laundry—and heaved the cinderblocks out of the way. He reached down, pulled the open trap door and they proceeded down the ladder.

2 minutes 15 seconds

When they reached terra firma without attack from any birdmen, Tommy began to feel hopeful. Buck and Tommy wrapped one of Allan's arms around their necks as the three men wove though the maze of slab casters and old blast furnaces.

1 minute 45 seconds

They exited the steel works a moment later and found themselves in total darkness. It was night outside, but none of that mattered. They were running now, as fast as

they could while struggling to shoulder Allan's bulk and
Tommy's injured leg. More than ever Allan felt more like
a sack of hardening concrete to Tommy right now than a
man of flesh and blood. Even so, the sound of the wind
playing gently with the leaves and the faint odor of pine
and gravel were better than Tommy had ever
remembered them. He was about to smile, hell, he was
gonna shout at the top of his lungs, when his ears caught
something beyond the rustle of leaves.

Whoomp, whoomp, whoomp ...

Both men looked up. A dark streak moved rapidly
overhead.

Their car was nearby. Another twenty seconds and
they'd be safe. Buck turned, searching the sky for it,
shotgun poised, but it was gone. Not entirely gone, since
they could hear it wheeling around, but it wasn't in sight.
Tommy glanced up, mid stride and saw the moon blink.
The flapping of wings grew louder. Buck raced ahead to
the car and was climbing inside when...

Whoomp, whoomp, whoomp...

A giant hand pushed Tommy to the ground. He fell,
sliding on the gravel. Falling alone. Allan was gone, he
realized sickly. Tommy looked up and saw the great bird,
flapping low to the ground, with Allan's struggling form
in its claws. They were headed for Buck. Tommy
scrambled to his feet, trying to ignore the excruciating
flare of pain in his leg, and shambled after them. Buck
stepped out and leveled his shotgun, but Tommy knew
he couldn't pull the trigger. Not with Allen in its grasp.
At the last moment, as Buck ducked under the
approaching bird, it released Allan, who went tumbling
into the Firebird's windshield. The car rolled back from
the impact, knocking Buck to the ground, bits of broken
glass all around him. The creature turned up into the
night, flapping its enormous wings. Buck sprang to his
feet, his face covered with beads of blood and fired into

the air. The shot hit empty sky. Tommy got to Allan first and turned him onto his back. He felt for a pulse. It was faint, but there.

"This place is going super nova any second now, Tommy!"

The sound of wings pushing at great big pockets of air made the hairs on Tommy's neck stand on end. He rolled Allan toward him and then pulled him back onto his shoulder. Buck started the car; the engine coughed, stuttered and then roared to life.

60 seconds

Tommy jerked the door open, slid the seat forward and tried to deposit Allan into the backseat, but the fat man wasn't cooperating. Buck got out to help.

The creature was coming in low again, its red eyes blazing.

"I'll do it," cried Buck. "You just drive."

Tommy scrambled into the driver's seat as Buck wrestled Allan's limp and unyielding form into the Firebird's tiny backseat. "This sonofabitch squeezed himself in here before, he'll do it again!"

"Buck, we don't have time, she's almost on us!"

Buck gave a final and desperate heave-ho and Allan's body flopped in.

"We're outta here!" Tommy cried and hit the accelerator.

Buck barely had a foot in the car as the car jolted forward. He grabbed the edge of the crumpled windshield and the passenger window to keep from falling out. He fell into his seat with a thud and slammed the door. The spidery cracks in the windshield webbed out from where Allan had landed, making it nearly impossible to see where they were going.

"We're going the wrong way, Tommy! It's back there."

Tommy turned the wheel and punched the accelerator. The car did a 180, sending a spray of dirt and gravel out in a stream behind them. Up ahead was the aluminum shack that Buck had come to pillage and beyond that, the road. A wild boom and the sound of tearing metal distracted them. The roof of the car was sagging in.

"It's on top of us!" Buck shouted. Tommy accelerated, but a clawed hand broke through the windshield, showering them with bits of safety glass. It latched onto the roof, yanking at it viciously. It was trying to peel the roof back, Tommy thought with a panicked chill, remembering the minivan, opened up like a can of sardines. They could see the stars now.

I didn't own a convertible, but I'm sure as hell getting one now, Tommy thought skittishly.

Tommy punched the brake and the creature slid forward and onto the hood of the car. They could almost see it clearly now, its red piercing eyes glaring at them. Tommy hit the gas and the creature came toward them, the force pushing it in on them.

3 ... 2 ... 1 ...

The roof of the old Keisel Steel Works opened up in a giant yellow ball of flame, spilling out its guts like an erupting volcano. The door they had come out of not a minute ago was sent flying off its hinges, chased by an enormous fireball and the great smoke stacks that had once sent hundreds of pounds of toxic bile billowing into the air, were now themselves airborne.. The blast's shockwave jolted the car and Tommy struggled to keep control as it fishtailed violently.. The creature was looking up at the roof, the roof where its children had been; both no longer existed. What had been left of the roof was now nothing but a memory, as were its offspring. When its head snapped back at them, Tommy could have sworn he saw rage in its eyes. Buck jerked the wheel and reached across with his foot and pinned the accelerator to the floor. He was sending them right into the aluminum shack. He was going to kill them all. Tommy felt the creature's clawed hand around his neck before he had even seen it move. The pressure was unbearable. Tommy's face was like a ripe tomato, filling with blood. Buck had problems of his own. The creature had closed its other hand around his face and was trying to crush his skull. But all the while, his hand remained on the steering wheel, guiding it toward a certain collision with the small hut. From out of the back seat the barrel of the shotgun emerged and fired a single blast into the creature's face. It reeled back, seemingly just as surprised as Tommy and Buck were as the car slammed into the aluminum hut. The last thing Tommy remembered seeing before the world went black, was a piece of metal falling, dividing the creature in half, its thick white blood spurting out at them from its lower torso.

Months later

Tommy cocked his head to one side. "I think it's gonna look great," he said.

"You think so?" Buck didn't sound as convinced.

"Oh, I know it will." Tommy nudged the old man. "Anything's better than that patchwork you had before. That roof was starting to look like an pair of old work jeans."

They laughed.

Buck turned around. "What do you think, Allan?" Both men were acutely aware of the off-beige prosthetic hand resting on Allan's thigh. It still took some getting used to.

"I'd have to agree with Tommy," Allan said. "The place was beginning to look like a junkyard."

Allan laid the prosthetic on Tommy's right shoulder, his hand on Buck's left. They looked like three men who had spent time in the trenches together; bonded by experience, brothers in arms. Above them, a half dozen men in overalls were working away. The old roof over Lucky Lonie's had been completely torn away and was now resting in a dumpster. The new roof was the latest corrugated steel and it was costing Buck a small fortune.

"I wish Tig were here," Allan whispered.

Buck's gaze lowered slowly from the roof. His eyes narrowed. The exact nature of his expression was hard to read, but Tommy wondered if the creature hadn't left the old man permanently changed in some deep, unidentifiable way. It had changed them all though, hadn't it? Buck's face cleared as his gaze returned to the roof. Tommy pulled Allan closer to him.

"We miss him too," Tommy said. "We miss him too."

FATHERLAND

Fatherland is my most recent short story. The idea of reincarnation has always fascinated me as I'm sure anyone who's read Malice can attest to. One morning, a story idea came to me while I was soaping up in the shower. How would I feel if I discovered my child had a past life? And what if that past life turned out to be as one of history's biggest sonsabitches? I mulled this over several times before I finally figured out what direction I wanted to take it in. Besides, I'd also always wanted to write a story about a pair of paranormal investigators who stumble onto something far more disturbing than they could possibly have imagined.

-1-

The rain was coming down in sheets and Thomson wondered if it would ever let up.

"Been crapping on our heads like this for nearly a week," his partner Brooks said, wiping the water off the brim of his hat with one finger. Brooks wore one of those snap-brimmed antique hats that looked about as beat up as the man wearing it, but his partner seemed to think it made him look like Nick Nolte in the movie Mullhulland Falls. *Cept we ain't detectives,* Thomson thought, gritting his teeth, *and this ain't L.A.*

Brooks rang the doorbell again, just as the woman answered.

She was slight and plump with soft skin the color of clean linen. "I'm so glad you came," she stammered, wringing her hands.

Thomson and Brooks entered and removed their trench coats. Threads of water collected on the sterile off-white tiles at their feet. Place almost looked like a hospital.

She took the men's coats and hung them up. "Don't you have any equipment? I mean, you did say you would run a battery of tests."

Thomson was the one to speak. "Mrs. Kesler, our first order of business is always to speak with the child.

Your claim is quite… extraordinary… therefore we make it a point not to rush anything. I hope you understand."

She nodded in agreement, although the look of concern on her face said otherwise. "I just want to know, one way or another."

"We understand," Brooks cut in. "But if it's any consolation, given what you told us over the phone, the whole thing is rather incredible."

"Incredible is hardly the word I'd use," she snapped and Brooks recoiled slightly.

Thomson shook his head in contempt at Brooks' blunder. Lack of experience was all it came down to. Kid was as green as a grape and about as soft as one too. Of course, paranormal investigators don't need psych degrees, but knowing a thing or two about the way people think can often be the difference between a paycheck and the unemployment line.

"Let me apologize for my partner," Thomson offered. "It was a poor choice of words. Let me assure you, if there's anything at all to your suspicions we'll get to the bottom of it tonight. Before we begin however, there is the small issue of our fee."

"Oh yes," the woman said and pulled a thick envelope from her apron. She handed it to Thomson who made it vanish into the inner pocket of his dark blue blazer with all the grace of a street magician.

"Now, Mrs. Kesler, where is your son?"

-2-

The three of them ascended the stairs while Mrs. Kesler told them what a wonderful boy Donald was. For a moment, Thomson almost felt guilty taking this poor woman's money. He and Brooks had investigated well over a hundred cases of supposed paranormal activity and during each and every one the pattern had played out the same. Brooks always found one more piece of evidence to bolster his belief that strange things did, in fact, go bump in the night. But for Thomson, every case drew him one step closer to the inevitable realization that Brooks was a gullible fool. Perhaps the perfect example of this was the case of the old man in Hardin County, Tennessee. The old hoot's name was Joshua Cosgrove and he claimed to have daily conversations with Albert Sidney Johnston, a General killed at the battle of Shiloh in 1862. So was it any surprise that the good general developed a sudden case of stage fright whenever Thomson and Brooks set up their equipment to record the ghostly meetings?

And then there was Mrs. Patel, who swore that her statue of Vishnu cried real tears of blood. Not surprisingly, when the blood samples came back from the lab reading Porcus blood, as in pig, well even that didn't seem to sway her one bit. Thomson was into facts, the colder and the harder the better. Brooks had speculated whether the lab had made a mistake. But gullibility aside, Brooks wasn't all bad. There were trade-offs, like his connections over at the local university where the bulk of their findings were analyzed, not that any of them had ever come back with conclusive proof of the supernatural.

The boy's room was just ahead of them now and Thomson felt an uncharacteristic prickle of gooseflesh crawl up his arms. He was pulling out a pad of paper and a pen when Mrs. Kesler pushed the door open. Seated cross legged on the floor was a boy, no more than five or six years old, his gaze fixed on the toys around him as the trio shuffled into the room. They had walked into a scale model battlefield. Lined up in parade formation were dozens of gray toy soldiers. The kind they sell in bags of 50 and 100.

"Donald," Mrs. Kesler said sheepishly. "Did you wanna say hello to the nice men who've come to see you?"

The boy lifted his head and both men winced when they saw the flesh on his face. It was pink and stretched into a horrible scar.

"Was he burned in a fire?" Brooks asked.

"Oh, no," Mrs. Kesler said. "This only started showing up in the spring. Nothing more than a thin line at first. We called it his lucky soft patch. Then it started spreading and that's part of why I called you people. The doctors have looked him up and down and all they can tell me is it's either a skin irritation or a late blooming birthmark."

Donald went back to lining up his men, as if he were alone.

Brooks flipped through the pages of his notepad. "Wound migration isn't at all unusual," he offered. "Ian Stevenson's work on birthmarks and soul transference is quite extensive."

More mumbo jumbo, Thomson thought. He was growing tired of playing games. "Mrs. Kesler, why exactly are you so certain your son is the reincarnation of Adolf Hitler?"

-3-

Her face blanched. Thomson felt Brooks' hand touch his elbow warning him to 'take it back a notch' but shrugged his partner off.

"You think I'm crazy, don't you?" she asked.

"No, of course we don't," Brooks said, tripping all over his words like a gawky schoolboy.

On the ground, the boy continued to play.

"Mrs. Kesler, right now all I'm seeing is a little boy who likes to play soldier," Thomson said. "There are millions like him all over the country."

The woman looked flustered and Thomson thought he knew why. She's seen the kid's fascination with war, noticed what looked like scar tissue creeping across his face and jumped to a ridiculous conclusion.

She fiddled with the strings on her apron, looping them around her fingers like tiny nooses. "About a month ago, I was cleaning the kitchen when Donald came up behind me, nearly scared me witless. He was asking where the dog was. I hadn't the faintest idea what he was talking about. I mean, we don't have a dog. I told him as much and he shook his head and became real adamant that he owned a dog and wanted to know where I'd put her. Said she was a gift from Martin, that she'd just had a litter and he needed to find her right away.

66

Wasn't more than an hour later that I heard him upstairs in his room, calling out for Blondi. I was afraid. I wasn't sure who he was talking to, but he kept on tapping his leg and saying 'Kommen hier Blondie' over and over again."

"That's German," Brooks said. He was searching the net on his phone, his fingers dancing over the tiny keyboard at a frantic pace. "Says here Hitler loved dogs. His favorite was a Shepherd named Blondi that he took with him into the Führerbunker." Brooks paused, the blood draining from his face. "She had a litter of pups right before she died."

"She didn't just die. The dog was killed," Thomson amended. "Hitler fed her cyanide capsules because he had doubts about the poison's potency." Thomson flipped through his notepad and poised the pen in his hand to take notes. "How many hours of television does Donald watch, Mrs. Kesler?"

"Very few."

"Does he have friends? Go on play dates?"

"Well, sure he does. Other little boys from his class mostly. One of them lives on our street, Samuel. You think he got this from one of them? None of them speak any German though, at least I don't think they do."

Thomson looked up from his notes. "The key here, Mrs. Kesler, is that you don't think they do. A child's mind is like a sponge, you see. You'd be absolutely amazed at the amount of raw data they absorb on a daily basis. Wouldn't take much more than an absent minded adult watching a war documentary in another room for that kind of thing to seep into Donald's subconscious mind."

"I want you to be right, Mr. Thomson. Not just for obvious reasons. I'm not sure if you're aware, but I'm Jewish and so is most of the neighborhood. I wanted this to go away so badly, but after the scar on Donald's face started to spread, I didn't think I could ignore it any longer. But you see, no one can know what I'm telling you here. Can you imagine what would happen? You don't know what people are capable of." Mrs. Kesler's voice started to rise and Donald looked up at her. "The Goldbergs were at Dachau, for crying out loud. For all I know, their son is liable to kick down the door and hurt Donald and I won't take that risk. I don't care what he was all those years ago, he's my son now. That's why I want you to be right, Mr. Thomson. More than you know."

Thomson's eyes fell and found Donald, clutching his mother's leg.

-4-

Thomson and Brooks retrieved their equipment from the van they had arrived in and hauled it up to Donald's bedroom. EMF detectors, temperature sensors, a portable oscilloscope and even an ionization detector. Donald sat on his bed, his tiny, pale hands gripping the superman bedspread as he watched the men set up their equipment.

Outside, heavy drops of rain battered the windows.

Brooks sat on the bed next to Donald and got him to lift his shirt. They needed to attach the suction cups to his temples and chest. Patches of skin on Donald's chest also looked burned.

"What happened to your skin Donald?" Brooks asked as he attached the receptors.

Donald's eyes dropped. "The fire touched me."

"You got burned?"

The boy nodded.

"Can you tell me when this happened?"

"I don't remember."

Brooks applied the last suction cup. "I need you to be still, Donald. Can you do that for me?"

"I think so."

Reaching down, Brooks scooped up a toy soldier and slid it into the boy's hand. "Just relax now."

Thomson had set most of the equipment on a dresser and was still fiddling with various settings.

"I don't think any of this stuff's gonna do us any good," Brooks said coming up behind him.

Thomson shook his head in mock disgust. "That's a surprise. I thought you were a believer?"

"You mean, do I think this kid really *was* Hitler?" Brooks asked, whispering that last part as though he'd said a curse word. "I'm not sure yet. I'm only saying we can bring in all the ghost busting gear you want, but I don't think it's gonna do much good. We need to talk to the boy. We might even need to call in Shrodder."

Thomson let out a dry laugh. "We need hard scientific data, not some whack job quack who specializes in hypnosis. You still don't get it, do you Brooks? We'll never be taken seriously unless we do things right."

"But at least Shrodder might be able to get some historical facts we can verify. Remember the James Leininger case? That boy said he was a World War II fighter pilot and how did his parents discover the truth? They called in a hypnotist." Brooks was shaking his head. "I think you've already made up your mind on this one."

"What are you implying here? That I'm closed minded or that I'm burned out?"

Brooks raised his hands in a kind of peace offering. "I didn't use those words, you did."

"At least I haven't turned into a gullible fool. Is it any surprise we aren't taken seriously? Every time we stumble onto a case you're so ready to believe that gullibility's dribbling out your ears."

"You crusty old son of a bitch! You think you're Stephen frikin' Hawking, don't you?"

Mrs. Kesler's voice came from downstairs. "Everything all right up there?"

"Everything's fine," Thomson called back in reply, drawing in a deep breath. "We're running a few tests, that's all." He could feel his heart hammering in his chest. Brooks wasn't more than a foot away from him, his smooth, youthful face a mask of indignation. In spite of their professional differences, the two men had never lashed out at each other, especially not on a job. They stood there for a moment, staring at each other, wondering what had triggered the outburst. Stress? Lack of sleep? Could have been either one really.

Both men looked over at the same time, and found Donald still seated on the bed, watching them with a strange glimmer in his eyes. The boy was smiling.

-5-

The readings on the equipment were coming back now and everything seemed to be normal. Donald's heartbeat and vital signs. Temperature fluctuations. Ionization levels. But Thomson knew Brooks was right. None of this expensive gear was worth a damn when investigating past lives. Perhaps, Thomson acknowledged, it had more to do with looking official and scientific. Had more to do with wanting to stick it to the critics and finally be taken seriously. How could they call themselves scientific investigators without scientific instruments, right?

Thomson would need to question the kid. He knew that. The boy wasn't more than a few feet away, watching them both, displaying the patience of a saint. Apart from a few odd circumstantial indicators, nothing they'd seen so far suggested they were dealing with anything other than a little boy with an unfortunate skin condition. *So why don't I want to speak with him?* Thomson wondered skittishly.

Brooks brought Donald to the kiddy table, where he began playing with Plasticine and Crayola crayons. For all his youth and awkwardness on the job, Brooks was a natural with kids and Thomson couldn't help feeling a little envious. Thomson pulled up one of the tiny chairs and felt his knees pop as he settled into it, not entirely sure it would hold his weight. Streaks of sweat were rolling down his face and he dabbed at his forehead with a hanky from his back pocket.

"Donald."

The boy looked up. He was rolling a piece of purple modeling clay into the shape of a gun barrel or was it a cannon? Thomson couldn't tell which.

"I'm gonna run some names by you and I want you to tell me what you know about them. Can you do that?"

Donald nodded. "Okay"

"Bob the Builder."

Donald's face lit up. "He hammers stuff." Donald swung his arm up and down enthusiastically.

"What about Thomas the Train."

"I know him too. I watch him on TV, with my mom."

"So far so good," Thomson said. "How about Strawberry Shortcake?"

The boy's smile disappeared. "I don't know that one."

"That's a girl's toy. See I was testing you."

Brooks was behind them, trying to stifle a laugh. "Guess I'm not the only one that doesn't get your sad jokes."

Thomson ignored him.

"I have another name for you. Joseph Goebbels? Does that sound familiar?"

Donald's eyes suddenly looked glassy and vacant. "I don't know that one either," he said, sounding as though he were miles away.

"What about Adolf Hitler? Ever heard that name before?"

Donald's eyes sank to the clay cannon in his hands and he resumed rolling out that crude barrel shape.

"Donald?" Thomson nudged him gently. "Do you know the last name I asked you?"

No answer.

"Maybe the kid doesn't wanna play anymore, Thomson."

"Let's draw a picture together Donald," Thomson said, trying his best to block Brooks' voice out of his head.

On his left was a bucket with more crayons and rolled up pieces of sketch paper. Thomson unfurled them and laid them flat across his lap. A number of them already contained images Donald had drawn.

"Oh, what a fine artist you are," Thomson said, hoping he didn't sound fake or condescending. "Is this a picture you drew at Christmas?" he asked holding up what looked like a row of blockhouses and chimneys belching black smoke. Thomson held the picture in mid air, rotating it, his head beginning to crane at an odd angle. No, this wasn't a row of blockhouses at all. There was a gate and spewing out the mouth of it was a crudely drawn pair of train tracks. The smoke stacks were also too high. And those powdery flakes tumbling to the ground wasn't snow at all, was it?

"Donald, what have you drawn here?" Thomson asked, although the question sounded more like a demand. "Look at me. Is this what I think it is?"

Donald stopped rolling his clay cannon. Their eyes met and suddenly the boy didn't look so young anymore. There was depth in the boy's ink blot eyes. "What does it look like to you, old man?" Donald snapped and Thomson wasn't sure anymore who he was speaking to. Children weren't supposed to talk like this.

74

6

"It looks like Auschwitz," Thomson said, feeling Brooks move to his side, looking down at the pictures in his lap. Brooks snatched them up, leafing through them one by one. Thomson's eyes rose and saw that Brooks' face had suddenly turned the color of bleached bone.

"What's wrong?" Thomson asked, not entirely sure he wanted to hear the answer.

Brooks fumbled the phone out of his pocket and began clicking away. A second later, after he found what he was looking for, he thrust the phone out for Thomson to see. "Look!" Brooks said through cracking lips.

Thomson took the phone.

It was a sketch. Some kind of church or bell tower. The image had a name: "Ardoye in Flanders." Brooks clicked to the next page for him. Another image, this one a painting of a crumbling cathedral called "Ruins of a Cloister in Messines." There were many others and Thomson looked over each of them before asking:

"What are these?"

Brooks placed Donald's drawings back in Thomson's lap. "Now look at the kid's pictures. They're nearly identical."

Thomson compared them, flipping back and forth between the images on the phone and the pictures laid out before him. Donald's images were very rough and drawn with a child's crayon, but the similarities were uncanny.

"You gonna tell me what I'm looking at?" Thomson finally asked once he felt he'd seen enough.

"Paintings…" Brooks replied, the ashen color of his face even more pronounced now. "Paintings done by Adolf Hitler when he was young. He'd tried to become a painter. I'm not sure if you knew that. Not many people do. He'd tried to become a painter and when the Academy of Fine Arts Vienna rejected him for the second time, well, the rest is history."

Donald had given up on the cannon and was touching up the picture Thomson thought looked an awful lot like Auschwitz.

Thomson stood up and loosened his collar. "I think you better call Shrodder."

-7-

Hanz Shrodder laid his briefcase down on the table and combed back a mess of graying hair that had the consistency of steel wool. Shrodder opened the briefcase and what Thomson saw inside almost made him giggle. A bag of potato chips and a dustpan.

"What is it we are dealing with here?" Shrodder asked.

"If it's all right Dr. Shrodder, I'd prefer not to say," Thomson replied.

Shrodder's left eyebrow went up in an almost perfect upside down V.

"We have our suspicions," Brooks cut in. "We just don't wanna prejudice your findings."

"I see," Shrodder said and laid a potato chip on his tongue like he was receiving communion. He must have seen the look of worry on Thomson's face, because a second later he said, "The salt keeps me alert."

Thomson nodded. "As long as we get some results, I don't care what you eat."

Shrodder crunched another chip and turned to Donald, who was still sitting at his kiddy table, drawing.

"This is the subject, I presume?"

Brooks nodded. "His name is Donald. We've checked his vitals and they all appear to be normal. Environmental conditions are also standard. We'd like you to put him under and see if you can find out any details of a past life."

"Uh huh." He turned to Donald. "Hello, young man," Shrodder said, eyeing the burn across the boy's face.

"Hello."

"We're going to put you under hypnosis and bring you back in time, would you like that?"

"I guess so. Are you sure I'll be able to come back?"

Shrodder smiled. "You're a sweet boy. Of course you will. Come here and lay down on your bed. That's it. I want you to lie down and relax."

Thomson and Brooks stood by the equipment in the back of the bedroom, listening eagerly.

Shrodder dropped another chip on his tongue and crunched it silently. "Now, lay back and take a deep breath for me. In and out. Very good. I want you to imagine you're walking along a beach. Have you ever been to the beach Donald?"

"Just one time."

"Did you enjoy it?"

Donald nodded.

"The beach is lovely isn't it? I want you to feel the warm sand between your toes, the sun on your skin, see the waves lapping against the shore. This beach is a kind of time machine. Every step you take will bring you further and further into the past. I'll be with you the entire time Donald, so there's nothing to worry about. I want you to keep walking until the scenery around you changes. On the count of three I want you to tell me what you see. One… two… three…"

"Blackness."

The sound of crunching as Shrodder popped another chip in his mouth. "Where are you?"

"I don't know."

The boy sounded scared and suddenly Thomson wasn't so sure this was a good idea after all. Wasn't sure if he wanted to know what they might find beyond the blackness.

"It's warm in here," Donald said. His body tensed. "I hear voices."

"What kind of voices? What are they saying?"

"A man and a woman. They're fighting. It's my mother." And the next part Donald said so matter of factly that the hairs on Thomson's arms stood on end.

"I'm in her tummy."

"What are they fighting about Donald?"

"Me. He doesn't want me. My father says I was a mistake and he's angry. You stupid bitch! What are we gonna do now? Get rid of it, I hope." The change in Donald's voice was abrupt and it made Brooks take an involuntary step backwards. "They hadn't really ever fought before I came."

"Move back Donald. Way back. Before you were in your mother's belly. What do you see?"

"A small grey room," the boy answered. "It's so very cold. I have a jacket on and I'm still freezing."

"Where are you?"

"In the Fuhrerbunker you idiot, where else would I be?"

Shrodder paused. "And your name?"

"Hitler. Adolf Hitler."

A potato chip fell from Shrodder's hand. He turned to Thomson and Brooks and for a moment, all three men stared at one another.

-8-

"What have you involved me in?" Shrodder asked, sounding like a man who wished he was back in the safe confines of his home, with the doors locked tight.

Thomson stammered. "We weren't sure ourselves. I mean, Mrs. Kesler had her suspicions, but frankly neither of us believed it was possible."

"I did," Brooks said.

Thomson rolled his eyes. "Yes, of course you did. There isn't much you don't believe in."

Shrodder stood on wobbly legs and for a moment, Thomson wasn't sure the old man was going to remain standing. He reached a hand out to steady him. Behind Shrodder, Donald lay on the bed, his eyes closed tightly.

Shrodder crossed the room and was reaching for his briefcase when Brooks spoke.

"Doc, please say you're not leaving."

The old man looked back, horrified at the mere suggestion that he should stay. "Are you mad? Of course I am."

"And miss out on this kind of opportunity?" Brooks cut in. "How many regressions have you performed in your career?"

Shrodder swung his briefcase into his other hand and rubbed his oily fingers along his pant leg. "Well over a thousand."

"And in all that time, have you ever met anyone who wasn't some no-name Ukrainian farmer from the eighteen hundreds?"

"I've not come across any Edward E. Lees or Elvis Presleys if that's what you're asking, but you don't understand. My parents and my brothers and sisters all died in the war, killed by that madman." Shrodder rolled up his sleeve to reveal a series of faded blue numbers, distorted by skin that had shriveled with age. I spent five years in Buchenwald, where I watched them fade away until the camp commandant had no more use for them, simply because they'd lost the ability to work. And you're asking me to speak to the monster who did this? I'm not leaving because I want to protect myself. I'm leaving because if I stay, I might discover if I'm capable of murder myself."

Shrodder flung open the bedroom door.

"But the kid's still under," Thomson protested.

"He'll come out of it eventually. Just let him sleep it off and hopefully he won't remember any of this."

When Thomson turned, he found Brooks already starting to pack up.

"What are you doing?"

"There's something seriously wrong with that kid," Brooks replied, wrapping a series of wires together. "And I think Shrodder has the right idea. Besides, without him what more can we do? And I suggest we don't breathe a word to Mrs. Kesler. She's too sweet a woman to torture her with this."

"Spineless chicken shit," Thomson mumbled as he sat down on the bed next to Donald. "Do you know that Brooks, you're a spineless piece of shit! You finally find

81

an opportunity to study the real thing and what do you do? You run for the fucking hills."

Brooks stopped at the door, gripping one of the portable oscilloscopes, looking like a child clinging to a worn out teddy bear. "You coming?" he squeaked.

The sap was itching to get out of here. But Thomson hadn't ever cut and run, no matter how weird a job got.

"Just because you and Heinz 57 there are too freaked out to continue, doesn't mean I have to give up." Thomson turned back to the boy.

"Suit yourself," Brooks spat and closed the door as he left. Thomson listened to Brooks' footsteps as they faded away.

Thomson took a moment to collect himself, then: "Donal– I mean, Adolf," Thomson stammered. "Are you still there?"

A deep crease formed in Donald's brow. "Who let you in here? I better not hear Linge put you up to this."

Thomson went over to the back table and pulled out his laptop from the remaining equipment He had a portable internet flash drive and he plugged it in, entering a search for the name Linge. "Linge was Hitler's personal secretary," he mumbled. Thomson returned to the boy.

"I want you to go back further now, much further. What do you see?"

"A drawing room. A young boy is playing the piano."

"How old are you Adolf?"

"I don't know who you're talking to. Who is Adolf?"

"What do they call you?"

"I am Ivan Vasilyevich"

Thomson heard a loud sigh and realized it had come from his own lips. The laptop was on the kiddy table beside him and he typed in the new name.

"Holy shit! Ivan Vasilyevich was Ivan The Terrible."

An hour later, the armpits of Thomson's shirt were soaked with sweat. He had run Donald through a parade of history's nastiest tyrants. Nero, Vlad the Impaler, Ivan the Terrible and many others. Some even he didn't recognize and eventually Thomson could go no further.

"How is it possible that one soul could have been so many badass sonsabitches?" Thomson wondered out loud.

The deep throated laughter that came out of Donald then made Thomson's scalp tighten; he stood up and backed away, knocking over the tiny chair he'd been sitting in and he didn't stop until his legs hit the table behind him. Donald was still laughing in a voice that didn't quite sound human.

9

"Who are you?" Thomson demanded.

The laughter grew louder.

"Who are you God damnit!"

The laughter stopped suddenly. "Poor silly human. Of all of man's creations, the existence of God has been your greatest achievement."

"Who am I talking to?"

"I am known by many names and I have taken many shapes. At this time, I am known as Donald."

"Why are you here?"

"I am a catalyst."

"A catalyst? For what?"

"For change. What else? Creation cannot occur without destruction. That is the only universal truth we know of. From supernova to the changing of your seasons, the scale may vary, but the truth is unwavering."

Thomson's eyes widened. "You're a harbinger. A grim reaper."

"We have been known in your mythology as such."

"And now you've come back as Donald to murder more innocent people, haven't you? Don't you think we've already been through enough already?"

"We till the soil to prepare for new crops. Death is only one of many consequences."

"So what's on the menu this time? Natural disasters? Ethnic cleansing? Nuclear Holocaust?"

"A tiny spark of evil exists within each of you. We do nothing more than nurture what is already there. The fate of billions has already been decided. There is nothing you can do."

Tears streamed down Thomson's face. He hadn't been a believer before, but seeing now with his own eyes for the first time…

A knock at the door. "Mr. Thomson, are you nearly done?" It was Mrs. Kesler. Thomson turned back to Donald's prone form and spoke to the boy in a hushed voice.

"Now you listen to me asshole. You're talking about killing my family and everyone I've ever loved. Hell, you might even be talking about stamping out the entire human race. I can't let that happen."

Thomson heard the door knob starting to turn.

"I'm afraid the course has already been set," the boy said in a deep gravely voice. "There's nothing you can do."

"Yeah, try me mother fucker!" Thomson shouted as he stood and wrapped his thick fingers around the boy's tiny neck. Behind him, he could just make out the sound of Mrs. Kesler screaming.

"What on earth are you doing? Oh my God, get away from him. You monster, get away."

There was a cracking sound as Mrs. Kesler brought Thomson's laptop down on the top of his head. Thomson's eyesight began to waver. Donald's eyes were bulging out of their sockets and the boy's face looked like a red balloon, a second away from busting. Just a little longer. That's all he needed.

Another crack and this time Mrs. Kesler shattered the laptop over Thomson's head, bits of plastic casing and circuit boards components raining down all around them. That's when Thomson's world went black.

-10-

He awoke in the hospital. His hands were cuffed to the metal bed rail and his head hurt like a sonofabitch. Brooks was dozing off in a chair next to him. At the door was a policeman with his back to them, guarding the entrance.

"What the hell happened after I left?"

It took Thomson a minute to regain his senses. "That boy, he wasn't human." Thomson leaned in as far as his cuffs would allow and he was whispering now. "He was the devil."

The change in Brooks' expression was immediate. "But Brody, he was just a kid."

"He was not just a kid, Brooks, open your eyes for once, would you. You weren't there at the end. You don't know what he was planning."

Brooks shook his head.

Thomson felt the bandages wrapped around the crack in his skull. "That old lady got me good, didn't she?" He was smiling, but Brooks didn't reciprocate.

"Do you even remember?"

"Remember what?"

"You strangled the boy."

"He's dead?" The look on Thomson's face was far from horror. He was happy and it showed. A strange sense of peace came over him.

"Do you remember strangling Mrs. Kesler?"

"What?"

"You killed both of them Thomson. They found you in the driveway, sitting cross-legged."

"I what?" Brooks' words weren't making any sense. "It was only the boy I…"

Brooks was shaking his head.

The cops were gonna throw the book at him. Thomson could see that clearly now, but somehow the thought of saving the human race from extermination was a price he'd been willing to pay.

Beside Thomson's bed was a hand mirror. He wanted to see the extent of the damage Mrs. Kesler had inflicted on him before he had… before he had made her stop.

Thomson reached for the mirror, felt the cuffs dig into his wrists. He used his fingers to inch the handle into his grasp. The bandages were the first things he saw, wrapped around the top of his head like a turban. Then the dried blood at the top of his skull and knew that was where his laptop must have cracked his head open. But it was the mark on his cheek that caught his eye. A long patch of discolored skin, pink and smooth it looked like a burn mark. The same one he had seen on Donald's face. The room started to spin and suddenly Thomson became aware of something dark writhing inside his guts. He wasn't alone anymore. He had thought by strangling the boy that he could beat the grim reaper, but he had been wrong, terribly wrong. That thing had been right all along. There was no way to stop it and now, when the world died, Thomson knew that he would be the one who pulled the trigger.

THE SECOND COMING

Richard Matheson's Somewhere in Time (originally titled: Bid Time Return) was wringing through my head the day I came up with the idea for The Second Coming. In Matheson's story, a guy travels back in time, via self-hypnosis, to hook up with a long-dead actress. This was the crossroads where my slightly sick imagination took a left hand turn. I began to wonder what would happen if a husband went back in time to save his family from being murdered. Magazines at the time were looking for short stories of no longer than 3000 words (about 12 pages) which may explain the length of at least some of the stories contained in this collection. There's something about the uneasy interaction between Jack and Dr. Sims that I've always found comforting and at the same time unsettling.

"Now, I'd like to go over this one more time."
Ten little words, that's all they were. But they were
enough to make the vein on Jack Barrow's forehead
bulge out like a great bloody worm. More than enough.

Dr. Sims recognized the sign of tension and leaned
forward, his teeth clamped onto the arm of his reading
glasses. His head—salt and pepper gray—was tilted
forward and when he looked up at Jack, his eyes were
three quarter whites. It was late in the day and a stream of
fading sunlight flooding through the window gave the
office a warm and lazy feel. The blinds were down,
turned open, cutting the room with vertical shadows.
One of these shadows was across Jack's eyes and
whenever he moved his head, the glare was just enough
to make him wince. He was sure this had been a careful
ploy, masterminded by Dr. Sims to keep his patients on
edge.
*Maybe so they wouldn't be thinking about the questions before they
answered 'em. May even find themselves eager to be put back into
their padded cell when he was through with them. The man had a
sadistic side to him all right.*

"Why'd they bring you here, anyhow?" Jack wondered
out loud. "To ridicule me?"
"I've already told you. I read your case file, Mr. Barrow,
and I found it rather fascinating. I find you fascinating.
The line that separates civilized man from his primitive
self has always been a subject that intrigues me. What is it

90

that makes one man a doctor and another capable of unspeakable acts?"

"You think I'm whacked outta my mind, don't you?"

There was a cool, clinical look on Dr. Sims's face. "I believe you're absolutely convinced what you've told me is the truth."

Jack nodded and the sunlight made him blink.

"You understand why we're here, don't you?" Sims asked him. The question seemed somehow rhetorical.

"You're here," Dr. Sims cut in before Jack even had a chance to respond, "because one month ago, you were picked up in Kelly Park. Charged with … uh …" He slid his glasses on and glanced down at the chart in his lap, flipping through a sheaf of papers. "Assault with a deadly weapon …"

"Assault ... listen, I was freezing … hadn't eaten in days. I'd come back with nothing."

"Come back you say to 'save your wife and kids' as you put it. Why then did you not go to the police?"

"Doc, we've already been over this." Jack's voice had gone up a notch and he saw the change in Dr. Sims's expression.

Jack knew there was a chance that Sims might end the session right then and there. In the handful of times they had met, Jack had seen how moody and childish the doctor could be, especially when he didn't get his way. But it didn't happen. Instead, Sims leaned back, crossed his arms over his clipboard and said, "We've had what, almost half a dozen sessions together so far, you and I? Maybe more?"

Jack propped a hand over his eyes to block the sun.

"And in all that time you've never offered me a single shred of evidence to support this story of yours." Sims held up a solitary index finger and to Jack it looked like a judge's gavel. "Not one," the doctor mouthed.

91

"That's not true," Jack interjected quickly. "I gave you the jockey, uh, Rich ... no ... Stanley Peck. I told you he was gonna win the Derby. That I did tell you."

Sims's face flashed with annoyance. "You did, Mr. Barrow, and he was favored five to one. Now, had you told me Longjacket Pete would have come up from the rear to beat a thirty to one, I'd have an easier time believing you."

"I never said I was psychic."

"No," Sims said. "No, you didn't."

"But you still don't get it." Jack's voice was rising again. "It doesn't matter whether or not you believe me, cause right now, while we're sitting here wasting time, she's getting ready to—"

"Who? Who's she? The one you say is going to kill your family?"

Jack paused. The throbbing in his head was beginning to make him feel dizzy. He could still feel the nodule at the back of his skull where the crowbar had connected.

"Yes," he snapped, looking over Sims's shoulder to the calendar on his desk.

"Eric, my son, will forget to remove the key from the niche above our front door. I'd told him it was the first place anyone would look ..."

"And that's how she gets in?"

"Yeah, like I told you a thousand times already and a million times before that ..."

"That's where you're wrong, Mr. Barrow. It matters a great deal whether or not I believe you, because it'll be with my recommendation that you get to leave Bellevue Heights."

Jack shrank back. "Goddamn nuthouse, is what it is."

"Now," Sims paused. "We need to go back and start from the beginning, Mr. Barrow and go through everything that happens. Just one last time. As if you and I had just met ..."

Jack was shaking his head when the thought of Chinese water torture came to him. He had heard the expression first as a child growing up in Cleveland. The kids had called his Uncle Sal "Knuckles"; he'd come back from the war in Korea with a real chip on his shoulder. A Chinese sniper had taken three of his fingers off at the joint and with them, what little sense of humor Sal had left. Jack always remembered the funny look on his face whenever he told them about how those Chinks used to tie folks up under big ol' buckets of water, with tiny holes poked in the bottom. Just enough for a drop or two at a time, no more. And how you were tied just right so that the water would hit your forehead dead centre, each and every time. Of course, as Knuckles told it, the first two hundred drops never did much more than annoy the hell out of you. At about the first thousand, the skin on your head would start to redden. And by twenty thousand, when your head was beginning to bear more than a passing resemblance to a soggy watermelon, you were telling those sick bastards anything they wanted to hear. In a very real way, this was precisely how Jack felt at this very moment. Forced to tell his story again and again, shrink after shrink. Over and over. Drop after excruciating drop. Jack's head slipped into the open palms of his hands. For what he hoped was the last time, he began telling his story.

"October 12th was when it happened. Little after two-thirty in the morning. A woman came into my house holding a crowbar. Strolled right in through the front door. Probably hadn't taken her longer than thirty seconds to find the key above the door. First, she made her way into my daughter Jenny's room and beat her so brutally the police found blood inside her Winnie the Pooh lamp shade on the ceiling. Then she went to my son Eric's room, where in a matter of seconds, his skull looked like it was opened up with a handful of TNT." Jack's eyes met Dr. Sims's and hardened. "From there, she found my wife's room and by the time the bitch was done with her, she was in pieces, along with my unborn son."

"And where were you through all of this?" There was a note of disbelief in Sims's voice and Jack didn't like it one bit.

"Me?" Jack asked, unable, even after all this time, to dodge the stinging guilt tearing at his insides.

"Downstairs on the couch. That's where I was. Look, I don't want you to think that everything was perfect between Susan and me. We had our problems like every other couple. Most days we were okay, but sometimes things got a little crazy. And when we just couldn't agree and it was between feeling lonely on the couch downstairs or feeling lonely lying in bed next to her, well, I'd rather have been downstairs."

Sims seemed to be enjoying himself again. "Go on," he said.

"I woke up with a start and saw that the TV in the corner of the room was on, just showin' snowy static. And I remember getting up to take a piss and seeing the front door swinging wide open. Well my heart just about leapt right into my throat. I rushed upstairs and straight into my daughter's room. It wasn't that I loved her more or anything, Doc, it was just that her room was at the top of the stairs. When I switched her light on, all the blood must have drained from my face. I remember my hand covering my mouth, trying to stifle a scream. I remember my fingers slipping inside and my teeth clamping down on them in horror. Then a muffled sound from our bedroom, like a steel rod whacking at something wet. Oh, God, my wife!" I shouted. "Not her too."

94

I ran into our room with legs that felt like Jell-O. The mangled shape of my once beautiful wife was sprawled on the bed, the curtains against the far wall billowing as if someone had heard me cry out and left in a hurry."

Sims was taking notes again and he stopped and peered over the rim of his spectacles. "But the killer wasn't gone, was she?"

Jack's hands were trembling. "No." His bottom lip quivered and Dr. Sims put a tentative hand on his shoulder.

Jack regained himself.

"She was behind you," Sims said.

Jack nodded.

"With the crowbar."

"Yes," Jack whimpered.

"You must have seen her then and called the poli—"

"No. I couldn't see a goddamn thing, but that bitch whispered something just before she hit me: 'This is going to hurt me more than it hurts you …' " Jack was holding his head. "Then she hit me …"

"Left you for dead, didn't she?"

"Yes. And for a long time after I wished she *had* killed me."

"And all this on the twelfth of October this year, you say."

Jack nodded, knowing with sickening certainty what would come next.

"You understand my dilemma then, don't you?" Dr. Sims asked.

Jack was silent.

"Today is October eight, Mr. Barrow. What you're describing hasn't happened yet."

● ● ●

"I know it seems crazy," Jack was saying. "Time travel is the kinda shit you see in those black and white science fiction movies. But if you check the Wilbur County records for a Jack W. Barrow, you'll see I'm not lying."

For the first time, Sims's face was almost expressionless. Almost. But Jack could see a twinge of contempt, wiggling beneath the surface.

"Find my driver's license, you'll see the resemblance. For God's sake you'll see

it." Tears of frustration were welling behind Jack's eyes.

"Wilbur County records, eh? And the address?" Sims's pen was poised.

Jack looked up, suddenly hopeful. "You'll—"

"I may," Dr. Sims answered with reservation.

"Two twenty-four Crescent Lane. That's where I live. Big white house with navy blue shutters. The eaves over the garage are bent outta shape. I was cleaning the leaves out a few years back … Oh, and the welcome mat at the front door says adios amigos. My wife thought that was the funniest thing she'd ever seen. But—" Jack trailed off.

Dr. Sims glanced up from his notes.

"You may see me."

Sims looked confused. "I don't—"

"I've come back," Jack said. "But the other me. The me that sees it happen is still here." His fingers massaged his temples. His face became the color of old ketchup, drying in the hot sun.

"Mr. Barrow, you don't look well."

"I—I'm fine. It's just that, going back messes something awful with your head. It's like shakin' a box filled with only half the pieces of a puzzle and hoping that when you peel off the lid you'll be able to make sense of it."

Dr. Sims adjusted his glasses. "You still haven't explained to me how you came back? In time that is."

Jack paused. "I'm still not entirely sure myself. I think a part of me is still back there, in the future, lying on my bed with that subliminal recording playing over and over. That's why I feel so …" Jack paused, searching for the right word.

"Fragmented?" Sims offered.

"Yes, exactly." Jack paused. "You know that feeling when you fall asleep and you dream of something you've wanted badly for so long?"

Dr. Sims seemed to weigh up the question for a moment. "I think I do."

"And that dream seems so real, you can't tell what's the dream and what's not."

"Yes."

"Well, this is that dream. Me stuck in this room talking to you. And for some reason I can't wake up. *I can't wake up*. I feel as though God gave me a chance to fix what went wrong and I've screwed it up." Jack's body convulsed as he collapsed into violent fits of sobbing.

It was dark outside when the session ended. Dr. Sims stood up—and when he did the joints in his knees made a sharp popping sound. Sims opened the lights and went to his desk, where he pushed a button beside the phone. A hefty nurse came in, followed by two men wearing white uniforms.

"Mr. Barrow?" the nurse said gently and touched his arm. Jack sat up with a start. His eyes were wide and disoriented as if he'd just been slapped awake from a deep sleep. They found the nurse's face and his expression darkened. His hands curled into tight fists. That's when the two orderlies stepped in and grabbed hold of Jack's arms.

The nurse took a confused step back and glanced over at Dr. Sims.

"That's all right," Sims told her, as the two men led Jack away. "He thought you were someone else."

● ● ●

October 12th

Jack was back in Dr. Sims's office, awaiting his decision.
It was early afternoon, but the sky outside was gray and
overcast. Inside, the room was dim, the corners webbed
with shadow.

"It's good news, I hope," Jack said, not entirely believing
it.

Dr. Sims sat down, removed his glasses and rubbed the
red marks on the bridge of his nose.

"Jack, I'm not sure where to begin so I'll just come out
and say it. I looked into what you told me the other day.
And in doing so, everything you've been saying has
started to make sense. I feel foolish, really, that I hadn't
seen it before."

Jack's face twisted with confusion.

"You were right. There *was* a white house at 224 Crescent
Lane with navy blue shutters. And it did belong to a man
named Jack Barrow, just as you said." Sims took a deep
breath and looked up. "However, on today's date, ten
years ago, someone went into that house and murdered a
woman and her two young children. Neither the killer
nor the woman's husband were ever found. Less than a
year later, the house was bulldozed. No one would live in
it." Sims sank back in his chair. "Now, is there something
you want to tell me?"

Jack's eyes grew to saucers. "Impossible!" There was a
touch of danger in his voice. "You're lying!"

"I wish I was." Sims looked down at his chart sadly.
"You killed your family, didn't you, Jack? You murdered
them in their sleep and then somehow concocted this
story of a crazed woman coming into your home. I've
notified the police, Jack. I'm sorry, but at this point, it's

out of my hands." Sims and Jack both looked at the phone on the desk at the same time.

Jack rose on shaky legs. "I don't have time for this, Doc. I gotta get outta here right this minute!"

He staggered menacingly toward Sims.

Dr. Sims leaned back and pressed the button on his desk. "Come on, Jack, don't do anything you'll regret."

A moment later, the door swung open and the two men in white uniforms came for Jack. He backed away, and one of them grabbed his left wrist. Jack spun and punched him square on the nose. An explosion of blood spurted out, hitting Jack in the eye, the viscous liquid blinding him. The other orderly fell in with his baton, smacking him in the back of the head. Jack fell to one knee. He could feel the plates of his skull coming apart again.

Dr. Sims was coming forward now with a needle in his hand. He pushed it through the skin of Jack's arm and for a moment, the doctor's face seemed to soften. Sims paused before depressing the plunger. There was a clicking sound coming from the back of the doctor's throat, as though things were moving around in there. The doctor began to speak, but his voice suddenly sounded softer, more androgynous, almost female. "This is going to hurt me more than it hurts you," he said, through a wide grin.

Jack's face was awash with bewilderment, quickly changing to horror and finally rage. He leaned forward to grab the lapels of Sims's jacket, leaned forward to rip the man's smiling face right off his skull, but instead he fell to the ground, his eyes rolled up in their sockets.

● ● ●

Later that evening, at two thirty three in the morning to be exact, Dr. Sims arrived before a large white house with blue shutters and a quirky little doormat. He glanced down at his notes and then up at the numbers over the mailbox: two twenty four. A smile played over his lips in anticipation. He reached for the ledge above the front door, his fingers fumbling over the wooden frame and then grasping the spare key from its hiding place. Sims had lied to Jack, more than once. That thinnest of lines separating man from his deepest, darkest desires was more than just a passing interest. No, for Sims it had become something of an obsession, hadn't it? And Jack had certainly been easy enough to fool. A little vocal gymnastics was all it took. Sims steadied his galloping heart and focused on what he was about to do. He couldn't help thinking about events looped in time and space. Even though it felt that way, this probably wasn't the first time he had murdered Jack's family and it certainly wouldn't be the last. Sims unlocked the door and pushed it open with his free hand. In the other was a crowbar.

THE BEARER
(Flash Fiction)

I've always been obsessed with losers. Or at least, the people that society perceives as losers. In The Bearer, I was exploring the idea of a man who doesn't look like much, he could even be your uncle, but underneath all the outdated clothing and bad hair was something much darker.

Baine was already through the doorway and halfway through removing his trench coat, when the woman noticed him. She glanced up briefly and then her eyes fell back to the book in her lap. It was something by Tolstoy; he could tell by the novel's monstrous size. The cover was cracked and the pages bent at the corners, but she handled it with reverence; as though Guttenberg's press had been dusted off and commissioned for one last chore.

She had dyed her hair jet black, he noticed. Quite a dramatic difference from the fiery red he had found rather sexy on the worn picture he kept in his breast pocket. She was also wearing loose fitting jeans and a mauve cotton sweatshirt, instead of the three-pieced charcoal power-suit he had admired from a distance throughout the trial.

D.A.'s had a way of all dressing alike, didn't they?

He didn't even need to check the creased picture to know he had the right person: her upturned nose and high cheekbones were a dead giveaway.

She woulda needed some serious plastic surgery to lose that.

Besides, a courier who couldn't spot his intended recipient didn't usually last very long and Baine had been at this longer than he cared to admit.

It hadn't taken more than a few seconds for the woman to become indifferent to his presence, though she was seemingly indifferent even to the sheets of rain lashing down outside the tiny café, drumming their fury onto the windowpanes, like something out of Genesis. But that wasn't a problem. Baine knew he would have her full attention in a moment.

He approached her, his coat slung over his arm, threads of water trailing at his feet. The aroma of French roast and espresso warmed the air. Baine's comb-over had skewed wildly to one side, like the convertible roof of a car, unlatched in the wind. He coaxed the stray hairs back into place with an unsteady hand and then wiped his palm against the worn breast pocket of his checkered blazer. This time, when the woman's eyes left the book and met his; she seemed to notice the dark circles ringing Baine's weary eyes, and more importantly, the eager look on his face. A brief moment of annoyance flashed in her eyes; polite disdain, as if to say, fat chance buster, I'm not interested, before a spark of recognition flickered somewhere deep inside.

She recognized him. He was sure of it.

A look of pain crept over her face, clutching at her expression like spidery fingers and Baine could feel the waves of emotion rolling off of her. Her face tensed, held for a moment and then crumpled. Dark stains dotted the page she'd been reading, circular patterns growing out from some central point. Baine glanced outside at the rain, and the notion suddenly crossed his mind that the woman had thought he'd come to ask for her phone number, that he'd been out to woo her with his threadbare blazer and bad comb over.

Slowly, the woman's face cleared and resignation replaced the sadness. She ran a shaky finger under her eye and drew the wetness away. Baine could tell she didn't want to receive the package and he fought to stifle the dread rising up within him. No amount of doing, no magical number of deliveries ever made his job any easier.

103

Judging by her reaction, she knew exactly what morsel of information he was about to deliver. Words were trying to fight their way out of him, but she snatched them away.

"All right," she whispered. "Let's get this over with." Her lips, soft and pink were drawn into a thin, delicate line. She set the book on the table, carefully keeping her place with a bit of napkin. Her movements were slow and calculated: a veritable ballet of precision. When her gaze rose to meet his, the silenced barrel of Baine's .45 was nearly touching her eye. One muffled shot rang out. The woman's head opened up and its contents painted the wall behind her. Baine lowered the gun and studied her, his head tilted ever so slightly. He might have been a sculptor or a painter, studying a work of art. His lips twitched and with the sleeve of his blazer he wiped a glob of blood from the cover of the book. He saw the title now for the first time: Anna Karenina.

A fifteen-year-old girl stood behind the register, her mouth frozen open like a sea bass at summer market. They were alone now, the two of them. *Two little Indians*. She had made the fatal mistake of seeing his face. She would have to die. The gun rose and as it did the color drained from the her tiny face. The smell of freshly brewed coffee was still strong. Overpowering. To his left, the lights on the display case droned like a hive of trapped bees. Baine's mind returned to the woman he had come for. Slowly, the gun fell away and slipped unobtrusively back inside his suit jacket.

Done what I came to do, he thought evenly.

Baine swung his dripping trench coat over his shoulders and disappeared back into the rain, headed for the cramped confines of his one room apartment, headed for the torment of another sleepless night.

THE GRIP

He had been alone for so long now that the sound of his own name had become a forgotten, dust-choked memory.

His eyes fell to his lap. The blood on his hands was still there; funny, all this time and he'd never washed it off. He raised a hand to his lips and let his tongue moisten a few of the dried flecks. Tasted real enough. But he knew better.

● ● ●

Cready punched the flashing button labeled "comm. scan one". Outside, a small and battered dish poked its head up and into the churning sand storm. Three labored beeps sounded as it peered up into the heavens, scanning the endless wastes for the tentative thread of a signal from home.

It searched for what seemed like forever before giving up. Cready's heart sank as the dish retreated. He glanced around, feeling cold and uneasy, feeling the very walls of the tiny habitat sliding in around him, twisting and snaking like the great muscular core of an anaconda.

He glanced down at the cramping pain at his side. The fingers of his left hand were curling, his nails pressing into the base of his palm, tattooing his flesh with tiny crescent moons. He straightened his fingers and held his hand flat against his thigh, until the muscles stopped fighting him.

Days bleeding into one another. He wondered, with no small amount of skepticism, whether this morning would be any different from the last.

Morning.

Was it even really morning? The computer's soothing voice had told him so when it had nudged him awake, but what if it was wrong? What if it were lying?

The display before him blipped and chirped. A detached female voice spoke to him. "Proximity alert, Lieutenant Cready."

"I'm a Captain, goddammit," he shouted back. He'd been promoted barely a month after arriving at the outpost. God only knew how long ago that was. The computer said they'd touched down a year and three months back, but it sure as hell felt a lot longer than that. Enough time, one would think, for the systems back home to have been updated. Truth be told, the promotion had probably done more to depress Cready than anything else. It sure as hell said a lot about CENTCOM's confidence in the mission. How many Generals back on Earth had promotions and praise heaped upon them when everyone knew they weren't coming back?

There certainly wasn't anything glamorous about setting up an early warning system—Earth's meat shield really—but at the time, this being the farthest stretch from home, there had been an almost romantic quality to the mission.

"Proximity alert, Lieutenant Cready."

Cready gritted his teeth.

A tiny object, no larger than the chair on which he was sitting, was streaking by, 35,000 miles away. Odds

106

were better than even that it was heading for that black void between worlds, he thought, with a chill. Certainly wasn't a supply ship. Those were enormous and wonderful and a sight they hadn't seen in a dog's age. This cold shoulder from Earth was starting to become a problem. In a secret corner of his mind, Cready was beginning to wonder if something very bad had happened since they'd left. Something unthinkable.

A non-synthetic voice made Cready jump.

"What've we got?"

It was Chavez, his engineer and the only other human within a few billion miles. The compatibility tests back home had given them a Class 1 rating, meaning they should have been the best of friends, or brothers, and maybe back on Earth they might have been. But out here, people changed.

At first, he'd blamed it on the subtle effects of the planet's weak gravity. But he had come to realize that it was something else entirely. Something you were hard pressed to experience back home on a planet bustling with nearly four trillion souls.

Inescapable isolation.

That was it.

To look outside, one would think himself perched atop a billowing sand dune in North Africa or in the middle of the Arabian desert. He'd think it, but he'd be wrong. Dead wrong. And that's where the problem stemmed from.

The tantalizing sight of a home you could only feel through gloved hands. A beautiful woman you could never touch.

At the center of all this was the HAB: men entombed, elbow to elbow; the cloying stench of old milk; the knowledge that every drink sipped or meal eaten had come compliments of your own recycled waste. All this was too much for some men. There were stories of failed missions. Atrocities. Outposts with bodies hacked beyond human reckoning. Three hundred years ago, they'd have called it cabin fever. Today they called it 'the grip'.

The grip had become quite an embarrassment for CENTCOM. And why wouldn't it have? They were perhaps the most powerful organization in the solar system, with near unlimited resources and yet they suffered a mission failure rate of almost 50%.

Rumors had been circulating for months before their own assignment, that CENTCOM was secretly conducting experiments on the feasibility of replacing men with moids. A day, Cready hoped, that would never come. He'd met a moid once. All man on the outside and all wires and gears on the inside. Damn near spooked him senseless. The way it had glared at him with those two silver orbs it called eyes. As though … as though it had known …

"Hey Cready." Chavez was studying the readout. "Ya look like you're a zillion miles away."

"Huh? No, no. I … uh. Visual tracking of the object should be online any second now."

"You done a spectral analysis?"

"Yes," Cready lied. Chavez could be infuriatingly thorough at times.

"Checked speed?"

"Uh huh."

"What about trajectory?"

"Done! It's all been done!" Cready snapped. "Who's the Captain here, goddammit!"

"All right, all right. Fine. So what are we looking at? Any word from the computer?"

Cready tried to slow his breathing. "No. But my money says it's the same shit we see every other day, meteoroids, comets, take your pick."

The control module shuddered and the lights flickered briefly. Both men caught each other's eye, an expression of visible concern passed between them. A tremor on Earth wasn't a big deal. Back home there wasn't much a slew of experienced hands couldn't fix. But out here, on the fringes of existence itself, there was no such thing as a small problem.

The computer's cheerless voice returned not a moment later, informing them of structural damage to the HAB's mooring. They remained still for a moment.

"Wind out there's picking up," Chavez whispered after a long while. "On Ariel 6 I saw a sandstorm rip open two HABs like they were paper mache." His eyes were wide, his lips slightly parted.

"Well, this ain't Ariel 6."

"I've seen the specs, Cready. These modules weren't intended for more than a six month stint on a surface like this," he said. "Any luck getting hold of CENTCOM?"

Cready gave Chavez a look. *Step on my toes one more time, I'm begging you!*

"Hey, why you so touchy? You been getting down on yourself again?"

"I'm not touchy," Cready answered flatly. "There's probably a solar storm that's blocking the signal, that's all. I'll keep an eye on this bird, you just gear up and check the moorings."

Chavez left the room, muttering. "I warned 'em a desert world can't give a HAB like this the structural support it needs. I've seen it before on other worlds and it's always ended badly. But those desk jockeys just shuffle papers, don't they? And who gives a shit what happens to the guys on the front lines."

"Stop it, Chavez."

Cready could hear Chavez in the adjacent room, getting ready, pulling at the heavy suit, breathing hard. "You read your history books, Cready, and you'll see."

109

He wasn't stopping. Wasn't even stopping to breathe.

"Goes back to those Babylonian assholes. Minute they invented bureaucracy was the beginning of the end, if you ask me. And the end is where it's gonna lead. Hell, for all we know, there's no one home anyway, cause they've gone and blown themselves up."

The very thought was almost too much.

They would never abandon us like this, Cready thought desperately, his hand curling into a tight ball. *We're too important. If something was wrong, surely they would have sent some kind of message. Surely.*

Chavez stepped into the airlock and sealed the pressure door behind him. Cready could see his helmet distorted through the concave glass of the portal window. His face looked twisted and demonic. Behind him, a hellscape of blowing sand and barren waste.

Cready undid the button on his collar. It felt like the temperature was rising out of control. Hot as a sauna, he thought, fighting an oncoming bout of nausea. The HAB rocked again and he braced himself. A second later he stood and was about to cross the room …

The computer's voice made him jump.

He's going to kill you.

Cready turned around slowly, watching the tiny room pulling away from him. He could hear his own breathing echoing in his ears. "W-What did you say?" He felt as though he were speaking into a vacuum.

He wants to be Captain.

"What are you talking about?"

You know.

"Chavez?"

He's left you no other choice.

"Stop it!"

He's so very jealous of everything you've accomplished. It's eating away at him, like a poison.

"Stop it I said!"

110

Kill him!

Cready grabbed the chair by the seat and raised it over his head. "I'm warning you!" Spittle flew from his lip.

Put the chair down, Captain Cready.

Cready hesitated.

Please.

The chair sagged.

Yes. That's it. Lay it down. Can't we talk like two rational beings?

"Being! There's nothing 'being' about you. Bunch of zeros and ones, wires and circuits."

If you let Chavez report it, he'll be the hero. They'll demote you. Send you to the mines on Sentari 4. Mark my words.

"Report what?"

The computer was silent.

"Report what!" Cready demanded.

Cready turned to the sound of the air lock doors sealing shut. Behind him, Chavez was struggling to pull off his helmet. "You got a report?"

"Huh? No, no report ..." Cready's hand was shaking.

Chavez looked puzzled. "Mooring integrity's steady at 100%. Weird. Must have been a false alarm."

Chavez was coming toward him.

Cready looked down and saw two words on the console's display: *KILL HIM.*

He covered them with his hands, a guilty feeling creeping over him.

Suddenly the console was awash in flashing red lights. The shrill sound of the warning signal made Cready's heart skip.

Lieutenant Cready, trajectory deviation. Security alert. Trajectory deviation.

"What's happening?" Chavez demanded.

Cready's brow was slick with sweat. Chavez was draped over him, greedily stealing his every breath. The room was closing in around him.

"Cready!"

"I'm checking," Cready shouted. He was studying the read out. He paused and his mouth flapped open. "That's not possible."

"What is it?" Chavez demanded.

"That meteoroid, it just took an eighty-seven-degree turn and increased speed by 3000 percent."

Chavez's face blanched. "Where's it headed?"

But Cready knew even before the answer came up on the display. Chavez was the one to say the words.

"Earth. Oh God, this is it. Open a comm. link, Cready, I'm gonna send it in."

Cready's hands were shaking. "N-no. I'll do it."

"We don't have time, look at the weather outside! You're the only one who can keep the comm. link open."

Chavez looked at the display and saw that the object was passing the speed of light now. His jaw slackened. Cready looked on, his body numb from the neck down.

"Cready!"

Cready didn't move.

"If you don't step aside I'll report *you* instead. The full details of how you neglected your duty. I'll have you stripped of your commission and working the mines of Sentari 4 before you know what hit you, I swear to God!"

An expression of recognition flashed across Cready's face. His lips grew thin. His hand began working furiously. Gripping at dead air. Opening and closing. Opened, closed. Opened. Closed.

On the control panel the computer was typing something out.

Captain, he's left you no other choice.

Chavez was still shouting at him.

DO IT! DO IT NOW!

Cready drew his eyes back to Chavez and a chill ran through him. The engineer's face had melted away. In its place was the snorting face of a horned demon.

KILL HIM CAPTAIN BEFORE IT'S TOO LATE!

Cready's hand cramped around the smooth surface of his coffee mug and he swung it against the side of Chavez's face. The mug shattered in two. Cready's bloodied hand clutched the remaining shard. He was swaying with blood lust like a drunk in a bar fight. The engineer stumbled back, hitting the HAB wall, eyes panicked. The room shuddered. By the time he righted himself, Cready was there, slashing, ripping away flesh, tearing at Chavez's face with orgasmic fury.

At first the flow of blood was incredible, never ending, but as it slackened to a dribble, Cready was able to look into the hole he had made in Chavez's skull. He had never seen the inside of a man before, not up close. He had expected a red mash of blood and bone and a host of unidentifiable things. He hadn't expected this. Wires, rotors and spindles. Two mechanical sockets moved artificial eyes until their silver gaze met his. They focused accusingly on him and then slowly they faded to pinpoints of light and were gone completely. The last they saw of the world was the horror on Cready's face. A horror that was now two-fold. One was the dawning realization that he was now alone, dreadfully and truthfully alone. The other was seeing Chavez's true identity, his inhumanity; it was making Cready question his own.

Chavez had seemed about as real as they came. At times annoying and petty. Other times forceful and courageous. He had heard of moids being used on asteroids for mining, where the duration was indeterminate, the risk to human life too great, and part of him knew that it was coming, eventually. But surely

113

not for a mission as important as this one. And yet the form sprawled before him proved otherwise.

He looked to the computer console.

"How many robots were sent on this mission?" he whimpered. "One or two, how many?"

The computer remained silent.

"How many!" he shrieked, but there was no answer.

Cready ran to the MESS-HAB and got a knife. He stood for a long time, searching his body, looking for the best place to cut. So he would know if he was one too. He studied his hands. Which part was expendable?

He seized on his foot. How important was a pinky toe? But the answer was already there. *Not important enough.*

Cready kicked off his boot and swung his leg onto the counter. The wind outside shook the HAB and nearly sent him flying. When he'd regained his stability, Cready steadied the knife over the smallest toe of his left foot. Chavez's blood dripped from his fingers and sullied the target. Nevertheless, he pressed the knife down until he felt a biting sting of pain. His vision became dim and blotchy and the world nearly swam away from him. Blood gushed from the wound. Seemingly unconcerned, Cready studied the amputated toe. There seemed to be a sprig of bone in there, but he was beginning to distrust even his own eyes.

What else, what else can I cut? What else!

He caught sight of himself in the mirror on the far wall and limped over to it, a trail of thick, clotted blood marking his passage. He turned his head from side to side. He was laughing now. There was a way, oh yes. There was a way!

Cready grabbed the top of his ear, bent the tip down, and then lowered the cool steel of the blade against the soft cartilage. He sawed in short jerky motions until the ear fell away and landed on the floor with a wet plop. He wiped at the blood pumping out of the nickel-sized hole with the white sleeve of his uniform. He strained to see inside the hole. He waited patiently. He would wait as long as he needed to. Finally he saw. And that's when he screamed.

● ● ●

Alone at the edge of the universe, long after the screaming had finally subsided, after Cready had been alone with the soft rhythm of his own breathing for an unknowable length of time, there came a sound. The sultry quality of a woman's voice. A beautiful woman, by the sound of her.

Hello, Captain.
Cready looked up. There was doubt on his face.
You seem upset.
"I thought you'd left me."
Why would I ever leave you?
A pause. Acute distrust as he searched the question for some note of irony. Finding none, his distrust gradually ebbed, and then dissolved altogether. "I know, it was silly."
You and I are the only ones left.
Cready's eyes slowly sharpened, like a man coming out of a long dream.
"Gone?"
Yes.
"All of them?"
Uh huh. Just you and I now. No one else to bother us, ever again.
Cready's face seemed on the verge of clearing, threatening a return of the old Cready, the take charge Cready. Cready the problem solver. That moment of uncertainty seemed to linger—an hour, maybe a month—

before his eyes dulled and became cloudy again. He slid back into his chair. His blood flaked hands resting peacefully at his sides. On his lips was the faint hint of a smile. A thought passed through his synthetic mind. "How long is an eternity?" he wondered vaguely. He wasn't sure, but something inside told him he was about to find out.

The Grip was my first published story for a horror collection called Black Ink Horror. The idea, like so many I have, came out of asking a 'what if' question. In this case: What if you suspected you might be an android, built to resemble a human in nearly every way, how far would you go to find out the truth? I'd also been reading about how gold prospectors sometimes suffered from cabin fever, after spending the months of the long winter season stuck inside. It made me wonder if the same thing might happen in a future where humans had set up small outposts around the solar system.

The Grip is perhaps my most misunderstood short story. I tend to try and leave things somewhat open ended and I realize that can royally piss some people off. But I never want to be accused of spoon feeding readers and, personally, I always love it when a story hints at a disturbing future without insulting my intelligence by bashing me over the head with it. Since I do receive emails from time to time asking to explain the story, I figured I'd include some of those answers here. I admit, some of the clues I dropped were rather obscure. Anyway, here goes.

Cready and Chavez were both androids, stationed on a small alien world with the mission of tracking objects (from asteroids to aliens) that might threaten Earth. After losing contact with Earth, for reasons unknown (and by keeping it vague, I hoped the reader would be left with some of the same disturbing questions Cready was asking himself), an already unstable Cready quickly begins to unravel. What I'd really been trying to discover was: can an android, built as a perfect replica of man, also suffer some of the same psychological frailties that beset us delicate humans? In other words, can a robot go bat shit crazy? And my answer was yes, it can. Cready was promoted to Captain and yet, much to his chagrin, the computer continues to call him Lieutenant. Only one reader has ever noticed the fact that as Cready begins to progressively lose his marbles, the computer begins to refer to him as Captain and during moments of seeming clarity, when the real world slinks back in, the computer is back to calling him Lieutenant. Built to last 'forever',

117

Cready finds himself at the end of the story, alone for eternity, with only his dementia to keep him company.

THE NEIGHBORS

After reading a book by Stephen King at 15 years of age, I decided to sit down to write a novel, hardly aware of what I was getting myself into. King made the entire process look about as easy as frying an egg. And in my bright eyed naivety, I began plucking away without a clue where the story was headed. After all, it didn't matter. Real writers didn't plan or plot, they simply sat down and waited for inspiration to grab hold of their fingers and the details would take care of themselves. The result was the birth of The Neighbors.

Needless to say, I got about a page into the story before I realized I was in way over my head. Writing a book wasn't nearly as easy at the big boys made it seem. It required planning and some thought. All I brought to the table was an old typewriter and the D- I'd received in typing class (yes, typing class. It was that or physics and the lazy bastard inside of me opted for typing. How hard could it be, right? In retrospect, it ended up being one of the best ill-conceived decisions I ever made. One I continue to be thankful for).

I quickly gave up the story, ripped the paper from the typewriter and stuck it in my top drawer where it sat for many years, growing yellow and appropriately discolored with age. Then one day, not long ago, I found that yellowed piece of paper, dusted it off and read what I'd written. Most of it was a bad attempt to emulate the master, but there was a kernel of something good in there. My style has changed since then, thank god, but I thought the piece was worth another shot and I decided to finish it off. I also decided to keep at least some of the Stephen King flavor from which it was born. After rereading it a few more times, I think the best way to describe this story is: If Stephen King and Steven Spielberg had a love child, The Neighbors would be it. And like many of my stories, I wrote it first and foremost as a quick, entertaining read that might just help get you through a long line at the bank, or a boring high school typing class.

-1-

The townspeople watched in horror as a blinding flash shot through the air, followed moments later by a deep cracking of sparks and intense light. It was more spectacular than any 4th of July display they had ever seen. It was also the third time in a row that the old Alistair place had been hit by lightning. A mathematical impossibility, some might say, but fourteen-year-old Kevin Anderson knew better.

It wasn't long ago that the first rumors about the new inhabitants of this strange house began to spread; rumors spun and circulated at the speed which seemed to govern all small town news – which is to say it seemed to spread at the speed of light. But now, having seen those unspeakable things with his very own eyes, Kevin knew those rumors to be true. But more than that, he also secretly knew that the truth, not the watered down version that would be whispered between the townspeople for years to come, but the actual events as he had seen them unfold over these last few sweltering summer days, had been far worse.

Slowly, the Alistair house began to list on its side. Then with a deep sorrowful moan it collapsed into a heap of ash; the last of the flames already dying down from the rain. Kevin wiped at the tears stinging his eyes. Paul Roberts was beside him. A man who only days before had been little more than a stranger; a man who, in that impossibly short time, had become something of a father figure to him. The two of them looked into the sky with keen interest. A single black cloud hovered above the town, more menacing than any they had ever seen. Already it was moving away, the edges wispy and quickly coming undone.

●●●

Three days earlier...

On Sundays, when Paul Roberts wasn't feeling guilty for ignoring that unfinished novel from hell that had tortured him for the last five years, he was walking through Shelby's blistering summer streets. By now, he had seen what amounted to every square inch of the town and firmly believed that he could draw a map of the place blindfolded. Invariably, his walks would bring him past Fred's General store where the good – if not most entertaining – gossip was freshly circulated.

"Strange things are going on in that Alistair house," Fred had said, his face tanned and hardened from 25 years of sitting on the front porch. That had been last Sunday, before everything in Shelby was turned upside down.. He was surrounded, as always, by a group of loyal and weathered old men just like him, who ate up just about any load of bull he fed them. Why, they still believed he worked for the CIA, since he'd probably forgotten to tell them he'd only been pullin' their legs.

"Town just ain't right since those folks moved in," Fred muttered, half turning to Dwayne Sheiks, a skinny

122

man, floating in a pair of overalls. "Where'd they says they was from again? Russia?"

Dwayne's jaw twitched. "Chekoslovakia, I think."

"Germany's what I heard?" someone else put in.

Fred waved his hand in the air. "Anyway, they sure talk like foreigners, and no accent I ever heard."

Paul masked his amusement by brushing a hand through his curly hair. "I don't think anyone's met them but you yet, Fred."

"Tell me about it. They came in here two days ago and bought twenty three pounds of butter. Nothin else, just butter. Plenty well cleaned me out. Even asked me if I had more. Then they had the balls to ask me when the next shipment was comin' in. Well hell ya, I'm gonna order some more. Ain't got nothin left." Fred leaned forward, speaking in hushed tones now. "Tim Ferrette over there at First Realty says those folks paid cash for the Alistair place. That's a hellova lotta cash if you ask me. There are only two types of people who can put down that kinda bread: the Queen of England is one and Bill Yates is the other – and both are bad news if you asks me. There's somethin' fishy goin' on o'er there I tell ya and its got hell's bells written all over it."

Dwayne placed an unsure hand on Fred's shoulder. "Don't you mean Bill Gates?"

Fred fixed him with a beady stare from out of the corner of his eye. "That's what I said: Bill Gates." He wore the incredulous expression of a man dumbfounded that one of his pearls of wisdom had been called into question. "When you go home, you tell Ethel to clean that wax outta your ears. It's blockin the circuitry or something."

Dwayne plucked a pinky finger in his ear and wiggled his hand as though he expected something to come falling out.

There was material here for his book, Paul knew. Oh yes. A whole town filled with it. The possibilities hadn't been so obvious at first. The half finished manuscript he had tentatively titled, 'The Final Days,' was still tucked away in the bottom of his desk drawer and a large part of him had intended for it to stay there. But this wasn't just a case of good old fashioned writer's block, he reminded himself. Nearly two decades of trying to write for a living had resulted in a crushing debt and enough rejection slips to plaster every wall of the three bedroom house he'd had repossessed by the bank, not to mention the loss of... No, he was done with writing. It was time to start something new, only what, he didn't know.

His mind returned to the newcomers and it was then that he noticed Fred and his leather-faced friends were staring.

Paul's eyes had dulled for a moment, but now they were twinkling, a reflection, perhaps, from the sunshine overhead.

"I think I'm gonna go down and introduce myself," Paul said, seemingly out of nowhere.

Fred was shaking his head before Paul'd even finished the sentence.

"You sure bout that?" Dwayne asked, fixing his overalls.

"Yeah, I'm positive. Loretta Hill came to see me when I first arrived and I swore someday I'd repay the favor."

As he curled one hand around the back of his neck, Paul caught the disapproving look on Fred's face. "Fine by me, but it's your funeral."

-2-

Less than fifteen minutes later, Paul pulled up to what was still known erroneously in Shelby as the Alistair farm. Once his mind had been made up, it was really only a question of working out the finer details. He had decided fairly quickly that he would bring them a nice bottle of red wine. Vintage. Maybe something from California or Australia. These might not exactly be the wine drinking types, but everyone had guests at some time or another and he figured most of those would drink red wine.

Most.

Not that he didn't trust himself to bake something that wouldn't send these poor people doubling over the toilet or scrambling to pack up their stuff and high tail it out of town. The image of it alone, however, had been enough to finalize the deal, if not give him a giggle or two along the way.

A waist high wrought iron gate kept him from walking right up to the front door. Inside, a darkened figure peered out at him from behind the screen door. Paul waved, but the figure didn't move. Another shadow, this one larger, blotted out the first and opened the screen door. It slammed shut and reverberated with a wickery snap. The man on the porch smiled awkwardly. Paul returned the gesture and raised the bottle of wine.

"For you and your family. A house warming."

The man dissolved and blurred, as a bead of sweat rolled down Paul's hairline and into his eye. He paused momentarily, blinking away the pain. The man waved him in and Paul pulled a hanky – one he had begun carrying at Fred's insistence – and dabbed his forehead. He blinked up at the sky as he crossed the short distance to the porch.

"It's a scorcher out today," Paul said, stuffing the hanky into his back pocket.

The man nodded and smiled, warmly now and not nearly as awkwardly as before. "They say tomorrow will be even hotter."

Paul noticed the man's accent right away. He liked to think of himself as a man of the world. Generally speaking, he might not be able to detect the precise locale of a person's accent, but he liked to think he could at the very least choose the right continent. But this sounded like some odd mixture of South African and Swedish.

Perhaps just to hear the man talk a little more, Paul introduced himself.

They shook hands. His grip was firm, but not overpowering.

"Tomas Olak," the man said and then motioned behind him. "And this is my wife Elena and my daughter Silla."

A timid looking woman of middle age emerged from inside in a flowing summer dress. Beside her was a blonde girl with pigtails and a white dress, stained brown at the edges. The woman began brushing at the dirt, admonishing the little girl in a language Paul did not understand. The little girl seemed oblivious. She looked up at him with two blue eyes the color of sapphires. And for a moment his head began to swim away from him. The man – his name was Thomas, Paul reminded himself

126

– put a gentle hand on his shoulder and took the bottle of wine from him. The hand on the shoulder, the physical proximity, all quite intimate gestures for two people who had met for the first time only moments before, but it did not leave Paul with an uncomfortable feeling, nor did it seem false in any way. The man's touch was warm and somehow reassuring, a father's hand on his young son. An unusual feeling really, since this man was maybe a few years older than him at most. None of them had spoken more than a few words and yet Paul felt completely comfortable here – if not a little warm still. Thomas seemed to notice this and an expression of discomfort spread across his face.

"Paul, I would invite you inside for a drink, but we've been having problems with the heating."

For the first time Paul noticed that, in spite of the heat outside and the hot air rushing out at him from inside, this man Thomas hadn't sweated a single drop.

Thomas laughed and Hellena joined him, smiling. Silla continued watching Paul with those blue eyes of hers; like two tiny oceans, one size too large for her head.

"We have tried to shut it off," Thomas struggled in broken English. "But somehow it has been set on full with no way of reversing it. The knob is missing. I have cut the breakers at night so we can sleep of course, but during the day we need the appliances to work."

Paul nodded and fought Fred's voice ringing in his head

Dang foreigners got everythin backwards. When it's cold they like it colder and when it's hot, well hell, that's when they jack up the furnace. Christalmighty.

"I detect an accent," Paul said, a little boldly – and nor was the irony of the situation lost on him that it had been his intention in coming here to set *them* at ease as

127

newcomers to Shelby and here he was, weak kneed and starry-eyed.

"I am from Bulgaria," Hellena said, "and Thomas was born in Yakuts, Northern Russia."

"Ah, yes, Russia, now I understand why you like it so hot," Paul said, and then coughed a moment later when his sarcasm, lame as it was, sailed about a yard over their heads. But the truth of the matter was that right about now, his mouth was getting ahead of him, the same way it tended to after one too many Tom Collins'. Maybe the searing heat was to blame. He plucked the hanky from his back pocket and patted his forehead again. Little Silla watched him, as though a pair of antennae had just sprouted from his head. Her father reached over and ruffled the girl's hair and pulled her close to him.

Not long after, they all shook hands and parted, with promises that when the problem with the furnace was resolved, they would have him over for dinner. He agreed and walked back to his car, noticing that warm tingle still buzzing in his chest and making his head feel like a balloon, about to float away. That strange feeling stayed with Paul for almost an hour, forcing him to pull his car off the road at least once on his way home so he could shake the cobwebs out of his head.

-3-

The pedals on Kevin Anderson's bike didn't turn quite as easily as they used to. Time for a new chain maybe. Or more grease. Kevin reached into the bag tucked behind his bike and pulled out a tightly rolled bundle. He cocked his arm and flung it with practiced ease to within two feet of Mrs. Aymer's front door. New chain or not, it would mean digging into some of the money he had managed to squirrel away over three years, from doing this paper route.

The first foreseeable problem was Ma. He couldn't let her find out; that money was supposed to be for his college fund, especially since his father had decided to pick up and leave town around the same time Kevin had taken the training wheels off his first bike. The second foreseeable problem was the sizable chunk of his said college fund that had already been set aside for the scooter he wanted. Correction: The scooter he needed. He had gone to see it again just the other day. Parked in the shop window of Motors n' Thangs; blood red and spiked with a silver bolt of lightning flaring down the side, it was a sight to make the flesh on your arms stand on end. He had been careful enough with his money. A couple more weeks now and it would be his. Sure, Ma would have a conniption fit worse than when she found out her favorite soap opera, As the World Turns, was set to be cancelled.

Up ahead, he could see the Alistair farm. Ma had once told him it was one of the first houses in town. A pity too, cause the bank had foreclosed on the poor Alistair family. More than likely, Kevin would have agreed it was a pity, if he'd known what foreclose meant. He knew lots of other stuff though – which tended to happen when you didn't have a dad anymore. He knew how to make his own dinner when his mom worked the late shift at Vern's coffee shop. He knew how to fix the lawn mower, as he had last summer, when the thing started making wild clanking sounds. And he knew that he was required to ask every newcomer to Shelby if they wanted the examiner delivered to their house. Jed Parker would certainly not let him forget that. In the past, his results had been rather mixed. Some shooed him away absently and others were flattered and happy to be welcomed to the neighborhood. But to Kevin, in the end, it had more to do with the two extra bucks he got for signing them up than it did with welcoming or shooing.

Kevin pulled up to the long driveway to the Alistair house, intent on filling his pockets with two more crisp ones. He let himself in through the black wrought iron gate and proceeded up the steps and onto the porch. A flood of warm air greeted him, reminding him of the time that he stuck his head in the dryer just to see what would happen – it certainly hadn't melted his brain, as his mother had warned, although it had turned his face a deep shade of red.

A flimsy screen door separated him from inside. Kevin knocked and the door rattled in its frame. He glanced around. There were no cars in the driveway.

Maybe no one was home. But the door… He stared at it. It was open now. Pushed in by his knocking, he told himself. Not a lot, just a crack, but enough so that he could slip in without ever having touched the door with his bare hands.

Son, tell the truth now, did you break into that house?
No Sheriff honest. Didn't break a thing.

"Hello?" Kevin called to no one in particular. The heat was drying out his eyes. He squeezed them shut and blinked them open. On a table by the front door was an electricity bill, made out to Thomas Olak.

"Mr. Olak? Anybody home?"

The kitchen was spotless. A thin layer of dust had settled around the sink. Looked like it hadn't been used in months.

Take something. A harmless little souvenir.

"No," he muttered to himself. Oh, he knew the consequences of stealing. His backside had been swollen for three whole days after Mrs. Henderson, the stringy old pharmacist, had caught him slipping a Baby Ruth into his delivery bag. His mother had broken two wooden spoons over his posterior, which had only made her more angry.

"Now you've gone and ruined my good serving spoons, Kevin!"

He wouldn't steal, not ever again.

Kevin turned to leave, since getting caught in a prospective client's house wasn't the best way to guarantee your commission. That was when he noticed the door to the basement, rocking gently back and forth. A streak of vertical light spilled out from behind it, growing and shrinking as the door swayed. There was someone down there. The man of the house, Thomas Olak maybe, fixing the furnace. In Kevin's mind, it seemed to add up. This place was so hot it was the only thing that could make any sense.

Kevin opened the door and started down the steps as loudly as he could. He wasn't interested in scaring the crap out of whoever might be down here. Two steps down, he winced. The heat down there was even worse. Almost unbearable. It felt like a rainforest; the air musty and thick.

He reached the bottom stair and ducked under an overhanging light bulb. It flickered on and off, shadowing the walls around him.

Around the corner, something was clanking. It sounded like his lawnmower, the one he had brought back to life last summer. Then he heard the other sound; the wheezing.

He knew that wheezing sound – or one very similar – painfully well. That rhythmic pulling and pushing had been etched into his soul. He had heard it as his little brother lay in the hospital, dying. It was the sound of the life-support pumping oxygen into his lungs. The Leukemia had gotten him, Ma had said. She had pointed up into the sky that night, towards the North Star. "That's where Jason is going, Kevin, the brightest star in the sky." At the time he had smiled, but it was more to please her than for any real comfort he had felt.

Warm liquid was running down his cheeks. He wiped at his face awkwardly. There was definitely no one down here, he was sure of it and yet he felt a strange twinge pulling at his belly, the kind of feeling you get when you look into a dark room and know that someone's there. The hairs on his skinny arms were standing on end. Just ahead of him, the furnace was clanking away, shaking under tremendous strain. There was something behind it too, something he had never seen before, something with

132

lots of dials and lights. It was pulling air in and out, just like Jason's breathing machine.

Kevin's eyes dropped to the ground. Littered around the furnace were over a dozen brown tennis balls; the kind you find, murky and smeared with gunk, years after the dog has buried them under the porch. He squatted for a better look. The ground was damp and smelled wet and rotten. Kevin reached out and ran his fingers over one of the strange shapes. The size was about right, but these tennis balls had coarse, wiry hairs and were terribly warm to the touch. Maybe these people were drug dealers. The thought made Kevin laugh, but his voice cracked when he saw that one of them was broken, the top shattered as though someone had smashed it with a hammer. Kevin crawled over on his hands and knees to look inside.

Go on take one.

He peered down…

Go on Kevin, show Sheriff Netty the drugs you found and they'll make you a hero!

But before he could see a thing, he heard the noise. From upstairs. A spring being pulled tight and the screen door slamming shut. They were home. The people were home.

Kevin sprung to his feet.

Footsteps upstairs, loud and angry sounding. He could hear muffled tones. They were talking. But not in any language he had ever heard. Colombian drug lords, he thought. And in his child's mind, he was growing more and more certain that he was about to die.

No, of course you didn't steal it, Kevin. You did what any good citizen would do. You brought the evidence in to the proper authorities. Sherif Netty'll know what to do. Adults always know what to do. The town will thank you. Maybe even erase your prior slip-ups.

133

He looked around frantically. His bike. It was outside. They must have seen it parked by the fence. But there was no time. He hesitated for a moment and then reached down and plucked one of the prickly objects from the moist floor.

There was a window by the far wall. Tucking the thing under his arm, he ran for what may be his only chance of escape. As he made it half way there, the door at the top of the stairs creaked open and heavy footsteps descended toward him; a loud voice accompanied it.

Kevin wrestled with the latch on the window. This window probably hadn't been opened in fifty years.

Heavy steps hammering down the stairs.

Please come on. Please.

His fingers were numb from the pain.

Whoever it was they were nearly at the bottom. He could hear them flickering the light bulb suspended from the ceiling, grumbling to themselves.

The latch finally gave way and he swung it open and scrambled through. When his legs were out, he held the window with one hand so it wouldn't slam. Kevin scrambled to the side of the house and peered around the corner. There was no one outside. A pickup truck was parked in the driveway, its engine ticking down quietly. His bike was still leaning against the side of the fence, just as he had left it. He bolted in that direction, not looking back even for a second to see if anyone had caught sight of him. He pulled it off the fence and ran with it in his hands until he had gathered some speed. He hopped on and the heavy saddle bags filled with Sunday papers nearly sent him swerving into oncoming traffic. His feet found the pedals and he pumped his legs furiously. Kevin didn't dare look back. He had read his Bible – parts of it, at least. He knew of Lot's wife and the way she had turned to salt for glancing over her shoulder at Sodom and Gomorrah. Yes, Kevin knew lots of things. He peeked down at the circular bulge under his shirt, hot against his belly and knew that if they'd found him, scampering around down there in the basement, messing around with their batch of drugs or whatever these things were, that something very bad would have happened.

And it was good that Kevin did not look back, because he would have seen a face looking back at him from the upstairs window, a face that wasn't entirely human.

-4-

Paul had decided against heading straight home. His stomach had started grumbling the moment he had pulled out of the Olaks' driveway and hadn't left him alone until he pulled into Vern's coffee shop, not ten minutes later. The elated, light headed feeling stayed with him as he sat down in one of the empty booths and grew to nearly orgasmic proportions when he sampled some of Vern's famous apple pie. The secret, Paul thought, might have something to do with that extra dab of cinnamon that Vern used, or maybe it was a touch of nutmeg. Truth be told, even his grumbling stomach had somehow felt rather pleasant. Someone had gone and dunked the whole damned world head-first into the lovely pond. It wasn't often that Paul wore such rose colored spectacles and a tiny thought tugged at the back of his brain, much too faint to be taken as anything but a light gust of wind.

What have they done to you?

He wasn't sure if his unusual sensory bliss was to blame, but he couldn't help noticing the waitress. Five different times she had caught his eye. Once while behind the counter pouring coffee and four other times as she went from customer to customer, a gentle hand resting on their shoulders as she made sure everything was all right. She looked a few years younger than him, her brown hair secured in a tight ponytail at the back of her head. She might not have made the cover of Vogue, but there was something about the way she looked at you, or was it the way she looked through you, the same way Katherine...

Stop it!

And as always, the little voice inside his head was right. He hadn't come to Shelby for romance or excitement. He had come for the same reasons that contemplative city folk often made their way to Buddhist temples high up in the mountains; for perspective, to put his life on hold for long enough to figure out where to go next. And what better place than a small town in Shitsville U.S.A. The kinda place where things change at the speed of molasses.

When the waitress came by with the bill – her white nurse's shoes splattered from working an untold number of hours – his last bit of common sense took a flying leap.

Stephanie was her name. He could see it on her nametag and her smile lit up the whole decrepit place. They talked for what seemed like an hour, until a fat man in a Harley Davidson T-shirt and an impatient frown drew her attention by waving his own bill and a twenty in the air.

She had a son, he discovered, not a little disappointed.

And so did you, once, asshole, that voice clamored again after a little hiatus. *And a wife too, don't forget.*

But that feeling of elation had already begun to fade. Even the apple pie didn't seem quite as good anymore. Paul took his last mouthful, drained the rest of his coffee in a single gulp and left.

-5-

Kevin whizzed by Jed Parker as little more than a darkish blur. Jed had been out for a cigarette. Wasn't later than two in the afternoon and he was already onto his second pack. He was the kinda man who was always on the verge of quitting when some big crisis would swoop in and save him from making the sacrifice.

Today, that crisis had nearly come in the form of a boy on a runaway bike. Jed's left foot was on the sidewalk outside the corner house and he jerked it back a split second before Kevin tore past.

It happened so fast that Jed's keen eye only had time to register one thing: Kevin's paper sack was still half-full.

Jed ran a few halfhearted steps after him.

"I better not hear that someone didn't get their paper on time, boy."

When he turned back, he saw that his cigarette was lying crushed on the ground. A final wisp of smoke rose from the fading ember.

"Now I gotta light a whole new one," he mumbled, reaching a stingy hand into his shirt pocket and pulling out a fresh dart. "I swear one day you're gonna be the death of me."

By the time Kevin looked back, Jed Parker had already stopped chasing after him. When Kevin swung his attention back to the road, he was face to face with the front side of a Nissan Maxima. He squeezed both brakes, already knowing it wouldn't be enough. The bike's front tire hit the side paneling and sent him careening over the car hood and onto the ground on the other side. He made three painful rolls, his bones thudding dully against the pavement through his skin as he came to a slow, throbbing, stop.

Paul Roberts poked his head out from the driver's side window and looked around for a moment, as though he had just seen someone up and vanish before him. People across the street stopped what they were doing. A few stood and watched. An elderly woman, her hair a light shade of pink, covered her mouth with a wrinkled hand. Nearby, a man with a New York Mets hat started jogging across to street toward them.

A plump woman behind Kevin reached down and touched his shoulder as he sat on the ground.

"Honey, you all right?"

Paul ran over and took a knee next to him, blocking out the sun.

They raised Kevin onto two shaky legs, the large woman behind him brushing the pebbles from his clothes. He had a long scrape on his left elbow and a nasty, throbbing pain there enough to match, but he could bend the arm and knew that it probably wasn't broken.

"He's white as a ghost," the fat woman was saying. The guy with the Mets hat arrived and stood oogling, as though he'd just turned the TV to something worth watching.

Paul's face was almost as pale as Kevin's.

"Kid, I didn't even see… you just came outta…"

Mets cap finally made himself useful by pulling the bike out from between the car's front tire and the splatter guard. It was wedged in there so tight a spoke twanged as it came out. Kevin's face squished up with the noise. He straightened his bike and started walking away. Paul followed, concerned by the boy's silence.

"Listen, you're in shock," Paul said.

Kevin started to shake his head and then stopped when he grasped the awful state his bike was in. The front tire, not three weeks old, looked about as round as a donut with an oversized bite taken out of it. Even the wheel frame was twisted.

An unintentional tear rolled down Kevin's cheek. This was his source of income. His livelihood. And worse still, the only avenue to that scooter he wanted more than anything. Now it all lay twisted and broken before him.

"What am I gonna do?" he mumbled to no one in particular.

The bumps and bruises he could take, but this. This was a disaster.

"Come on," Paul said, motioning Kevin into the car. "I'll take you home at least."

Paul popped his trunk and slid the remains of the bike inside, over his spare tire.

Against his mother's voice ringing dimly in his ear – 'don't ever take a ride from a stranger' - Kevin got in.

For most of the way home, Kevin stared out the window, watching the passing trees and houses with little interest. Only after repeated inquiry did Paul at last discover where he was headed. The east side of town. 'Getsville', as it was called, since it was the closest thing Shelby had to a ghetto.

When they pulled into his driveway, Kevin leaned over to open the car door and then froze. He grabbed his belly, patted himself down briefly and then swore.

"We have to go back," Kevin said. "I dropped something."

Paul was looking out at Kevin's house: paint peeling and cracked; a shutter broken and swaying slightly in the soft summer breeze.

"Mr. Roberts can you bring me b–"

Paul turned.

"My name. How do you know my name?"

Kevin was quiet for a moment.

"Everyone in Shelby knows about you." Kevin fiddled with the door handle.

"You're the guy who lost his family."

Paul's face solidified: three parts anger, one part shock. Slowly the anger began to dissolve, leaving his mouth formed into a perfect 'o'. "I haven't told any…How…?"

"That's not true Mr. Roberts. You told Mrs. Loretta Hill. You tell Mrs. Hill anything that meets her fancy and in less time than it takes to click your heels three times, the whole town's gonna know. That's just how it works around here."

Paul's lips tightened into what his brain told him was a smile, but was in actuality a grimace.

"Now could you take me back, I forgot s–"

Paul reached down under the seat and came up with what looked like a large furry acorn.

"This what you forgot?" Paul asked, turning the thing over in his hands.

Now it was Kevin's turn to be surprised. But not just by the fact that Paul had snagged the thing after his accident. What surprised him most, was that it had grown. It no longer looked like a dirty tennis ball. The thing was much bigger and shaped like a giant acorn. Kevin could even feel heat radiating from it.

Paul eyed him. "You wanna tell me what this is?"

Kevin grabbed it from him. "I'm not sure yet. That's what I gotta figure out."

141

They got out of the car and Paul carried what remained of Kevin's bike into the garage.

"I know we writers are supposed to pretend we know everything," Paul said, "but I've never seen anything like that before. Where'd you find it?"

Kevin flicked the automatic garage door switch. "Found it over by the landfill."

The door closed and for a moment they were in darkness. When Kevin turned on the light, Paul was standing next to him, he was tapping at it with his finger, a worried look on his face. He looked down at Kevin.

"This could be a baby raccoon you know?"

Kevin exploded in laugher so hard he nearly dropped it. "Raccoon, hatched from an egg. Yeah, good one."

Paul wasn't laughing. And neither was Kevin when he caught sight of his bike again.

"Look, I can help you fix your bike," Paul offered. "It's the least I can do. Listen, tomorrow I'll bring over some tools and a new wheel and we'll get her up and running."

Kevin waved him away with his free hand, flashing a long gash which ran from his pinky to his wrist. "No. I'm used to fixin' stuff on my own."

"No, I insist."

'Really I'm—"

"I won't take no for an answer."

Kevin sighed. "O.K. Mr. Roberts, have it your way."

"I will," Paul said and then smiled. "Name's Paul,"

Kevin returned the gesture. "Okay Paul."

Paul brushed a hand through his hair. Something about this kid reminded him a lot of his son, Tobey. The Tobemeister. Not that physically they were anything alike. Of course, his son had suffered from a rare birth defect which had left him in constant crippling pain, but the kid would rarely admit it. Tobey got his pills every day and continued getting them long after they were no longer quite enough. No, Kevin reminded him a lot of his son. A little too much maybe.

He watched as Kevin sat the acorn sized object on a large cushion by his night table.

"Hey look at this," the boy said and opened the cedar chest at the foot of his bed, shifting things around, as carefully as a curator perusing through a collection of antiquities. He emerged with a comic book wrapped in clear plastic, a piece of cardboard stuck down the back.

Flash Gordon #2, in nearly mint condition.

Paul's eyes widened. "Wow, this must be worth a fortune. Shouldn't show it off to anyone, they might try to steal it from you."

The pride in Kevin's eyes flickered a little and then returned as he replaced the comic in the cedar chest.

Kevin's son Tobey had a similar chest made from unfinished pine. Paul could still smell the musty odor it gave off. And the hinge. For some inexplicable reason he would never forget how the right hinge had snapped off, making the cover open at a weird angle.

"He's in constant pain, Paul. That's no way for anyone to live." It was Katherine. She was before him in their bedroom, frozen in the act of undoing her silk blouse.

"You don't think I know? What do you want me to do about it?"

Katherine's hands were still pulling at the edges of her blouse. "His pills aren't working anymore, Paul. The pain... it's there all the time now."

Paul took a step forward. "Would you please lower your voice—"

"No, I will not lower my voice. You promised me coming home from the hospital that we would do everything in our power to make him as comfortable as we could."

143

"Kat, it tears me up inside to see him suffer, but a higher dosage is only gonna kill him. Is that what you want? Or better yet, maybe we should just whack him over the head with a shovel. Or stick a pillow over his face. Hell, there's nothing he could do to stop us. Maybe that would make you happy." Paul's hands were perched on both hips and then slowly slipped into his pockets. "Kat, I'm sorry. Look, stop crying. I didn't mean what I said…"

A small hand was tapping Paul on the shoulder. He had been looking blankly at a corkboard plastered with newspaper clippings.

UFO Over Norfolk.
Aliens land in schoolyard and warn of impending apocalypse.
24 Paluski residents witness strange lights in the night ski.

Paul pointed to the last one. "Paluski's not fifty miles from here." He leaned in for a better look. "You believe in this stuff?"

"Sure. Don't you?"

"I suppose I used to, as a kid."

"Twenty four people saw those lights Mr. R– I mean Paul. Twenty four. Twenty four people, all saying the same thing."

"Yeah, I guess they did. That many people can't be wrong, right?"

Kevin nodded in agreement.

Paul took a final glance at the corkboard and then headed downstairs. He wrote his number on a scrap of paper and handed it to Kevin.

"I want you to call me if you need anything. Anything at all."

-6-

To say that his mother was upset with him when Kevin answered the phone would have been the biggest understatement of his young life. To say that she was pissed, irate or even infuriated would likewise have fallen short of the mark. Kevin's mother, a patient woman even by her own account, was now in a white hot rage. She had gone thermo-nuclear. Nitro glycerin in a paint shaking machine. Kevin pulled the phone away from his ear and looked at it. When he replaced it, there was only her heavy breathing, devoid of the rattle which accompanied her lifetime of smoking. An absence that would only occur to him much later.

"Have you heard a word I've been saying?"

"Yeah. Kinda."

"Sheriff Netty came by the diner today..."

Kevin's hand flew to his mouth.

"Those new folks over at the Alistair place say you stole something of theirs. They say that if you bring it back right away they'll drop the charges."

Charges.

The thought reverberated through his head like a bag of marbles, cut loose on a swaying ship.

"Whatever it is you stole, I don't care." His mother's voice suddenly had an icy quality to it. "But for Chrix sake, you're gonna get on your bike and take back whatever it was that you stole. You do that and we'll forget this ever happened."

The line was deathly quiet for several agonizing moments, as Kevin contemplated how to tell his mother that there wasn't a bike anymore.

"Kevin, will you do that?"

Finally. "Yes."

"Good, go do it right now."

"It was a mistake Ma, really. I only took it cause I thought...I thought it was..." Kevin's voice trailed off.

"What honey, what did you think it was?"

"Nothing. I'll bring it back."

"Kevin."

"Yes?

"Your mother loves you." And with that the line clicked dead.

Kevin headed back to his room, his guts still in a mess, his head swimming. But another sensation had begun swelling within him as he'd hung up the phone. It was so out of place he couldn't put his finger on where exactly it had come from. He was feeling elated. He assumed it had a lot to do with the thought of finally getting rid of that nasty acorn. It had spooked him right from the start and in some weird way, he was almost pleased now that his little ruse had been discovered. He just wasn't sure how he was gonna face those people. He hoped the Olaks were understanding. He hoped they weren't drug dealers.

Then, as Kevin climbed the stairs and went into his room, that sense of mild elation turned to panic.

It's gone.

Kevin stood, his feet frozen in two blocks of ice. With gargantuan effort he turned and walked from his room back into the hallway and then reentered it, hoping to reset the minor visual glitch. He saw his bed spread

146

and the indentation where the object had sat perched. But there was no acorn. Reaching down, Kevin lifted the spread and noticed that something wet was touching his foot. Yellow mucous dripped from the side of the night table and into a puddle around Kevin's sock. He dabbed at it and then rubbed the sticky substance between his first finger and his thumb. The acorn had fallen somehow. But what could have knocked it over?

Kevin lowered himself on all fours. Judging by the trail of yellow goo, it was under his bed. He peered into the gloom and there he found it, lying on its side. He blinked long and hard. The thing was huge, pressing up against the underside of his mattress.

He reached a hand out to retrieve it and quickly stopped.

The acorn hadn't fallen over and rolled harmlessly under his bed.

It had hatched.

-7-

The words "Code Red" kept flashing inside Kevin's head. He saw it playing out before him. His mother coming home from a long day at work. She would invariably be tired and circumstances being what they were, still a little pissed off to boot. She would ask Kevin if he had returned what he had stolen and then maybe, if Vern hadn't been too frisky with her, she might even ask how his day had gone. Afterwards, she would slog upstairs, undoing her hair as she went, intent on drawing herself a nice hot bath. And within five minutes that peaceful silence would be shattered when she came tearing from the bathroom, shrieking that a wild creature had come at her from behind the toilet bowl.

Kevin didn't know what the hell this thing was. But he knew well enough that if Ma came home and it – whatever *it* was – was still in the house, he could kiss that scooter goodbye. Hell, he could probably kiss his life goodbye. He ran down to the kitchen and pulled out a pair of oven mitts. They would serve nicely, in case this raccoon or whatever it was tried to swipe at him. He was sneaking through the living room, just past the Victorian clock Ma had gotten from her inheritance, when he heard a low rumbling coming from upstairs. He traced the sound as he crept along the edge of each riser, one by one. He arrived at the top stair and listened. It was coming from his mother's room. Her door was ajar – and if there was one thing his mother was uptight about, it was closing doors. He pawed the door open and the rumbling grew louder.

When the door hit the whicker laundry basket, Kevin jumped. His hands were sweating something awful in the oven mitts. The rumbling grew louder. As though the Tasmanian Devil himself was burrowing a hole in her bedroom wall. He drew closer. It was coming from his mother's chest of drawers. Kevin opened the drawer and his eyes grew wide. His mother's "do–not–touch–under–any–circumstances" device was vibrating like mad. The smell of overheated batteries was strong and left an acidic smell in the air. Kevin swung around. The numbers on the digital alarm clock his mother kept beside her bed were flipping by at a dizzying speed. Kevin's head began to reel. He felt as though his mind was trapped in some state of suspended animation, while the world around him was going at the speed of light. The TV at the foot of the bed turned on. There was snowy static at first and then a collage of bizarre images: indescribable colors; odd shapes swirling; wispy clouds, long and drawn out; lightning; and then burnt paper, billowing through the air.

What the hell is…

Silence.

The vibrator, the television, even the alarm clock became quiet.

"Hello?" Kevin called out.

The television flickered on again. A nondescript face appeared, smiling out at him.

He stared at it for what felt like an eternity, goose bumps trailing up and down the length of his arms.

149

"Hello?" Kevin repeated, more of a question this time than a greeting.

The face on the television screen mouthed Kevin's words back to him, soundlessly.

"Who are you?" he asked.

The lips on the screen moved in sync with his own.

He searched his pockets for something to eat. Nothing. "Are you hungry?"

A strangled noise rose up from the set. To Kevin's ears it sounded a lot like "Rarou unny."

"You're hungry?"

"Rou unny"

"Is that a yes?"

"Tata-s"

It's copying me. Repeating everything I say, or at least it's trying to.

"I-I'm getting you something to eat." Kevin stammered. "You like peanut butter?"

The face on the television smiled back at him.

"You don't have allergies do you? Oh, never mind. Just stay here. I'll be right back."

Kevin raced downstairs and slid halfway across the kitchen floor on his stocking feet. He lathered some peanut butter onto a piece of bread and filled a bowl with water. He charged back up the stairs and into his mother's room and placed the two items in front of the television. The face looked down at them and grimaced.

Just then the TV flickered off. Kevin stepped back. From under the shiny chrome TV stand, below a stack of TV guide magazines, a tiny hand emerged. The fingers were long and slender, hooking at the ends like a chicken's foot. The skin was dark and scaly. Kevin held out the sandwich and the tiny hand snatched it from him and disappeared back behind the TV stand.

Kevin nudged the bowl under as well. "Peanut butter's real sticky, you're gonna need some of this to wash it down." In it went, as though pulled by a powerful magnet, only to be followed by the sound of loud slurping. "You sure are a hungry little guy." Kevin jumped a second later when the bowl, now empty, came spinning back at him.

On the TV, that gentle face was back, smiling contentedly.

"You had enough to eat?"

"Ru hada nuf toheet?" the voice mimicked him from the snowy screen. Kevin pulled out his cell phone to see what time it was. But that strange looking face was there too.

From downstairs came the sound of a door opening and closing.

"Oh, no," he spat. "Ma's home."

-8-

Paul was in the Shelby Public Library, going through the old town records, doing his best to do the kind of research that could take his novel to the next level. Authenticity and relatability. Those were the things his fans loved most about his work. At least according to his agent, Steve Goldman. Authentability, Steve called it. Didn't make a whole lot of sense to Paul back then, but now that he was in Shelby, the capital of authentability, it finally seemed to be making sense.

His novel, 'The Final Days' was going to be about a series of country folk in the 1800s, banding together in the face of a biblical style apocalypse. With that in mind, he was skimming through old family records and newspaper clippings on the library's microfiche reader. But all he was really doing, was trying to put some space between himself and the guilt he felt for nearly killing that kid. Kevin was his name. A nice kid too, who hadn't done a thing to make him feel like the asshole he was, for nearly squashing his head under the front tire of his car.

Paul was still scrolling, rather robotically, when his fingers jerked to a full stop. He rolled back a few pages and sat up straight, trying to ignore the tingling sensation crawling up the back of his neck. A clipping about a family of homesteaders. The McGary family, 1873. That's what he was transfixed on. Mother, father and a little girl with a pair of eyes that pierced a burning hole through the black and white newspaper image he was staring at. He'd seen those eyes before. Hell he'd seen that face before. Paul scanned over the parents and let out an audible gasp. These homesteaders, dead now for well over a hundred years, were absolute dead ringers for the Olaks.

That strange feeling Paul remembered coursing through his body after he'd met with the Olaks this afternoon came back to him now with full force. But what did it mean?

Could they be the Olaks' descendants? But the family names were different and besides, if that were true, the three of them wouldn't look like doppelgangers. Two out of three maybe. But mother, father and daughter? Never.

Paul pulled up the microfiche for Shelby cemetery and scrolled through until he found the plot that belonged to the McGarys. He tapped on the screen, whispering to himself. "What on earth is going on here?"

●●●

The cemetery was run by a white haired and pudgy little man named Tim Sheppard, who might just have had the highest voice Paul had ever heard come from a man in his life. If he had rung him on the phone before showing up, he very well may have called him ma'am.

Tim led Paul out to the crypt where the McGary family was buried. All three McGarys had died of typhus in the winter of 1876; it was there that Paul's theory that the Olaks were somehow descendants had withered and been laid to rest. The structure itself was simple and yet still impressive. Stone pillars out front. A solid oak door, with metal lattice work. Paul was in the middle of asking how a simple farmer could have afforded such a fine tomb, when he caught the strange look on Tim's face.

"Is there something wrong?" Paul asked.

Tim approached the crypt door and pulled it open.

"That's strange," Tim whispered in his sing-song voice. "This should be locked."

-9-

Kevin and his mother were in the kitchen and her mood had improved quite a bit since their conversation earlier in the day. When he'd heard her come home, Kevin realized there wasn't any time to flush his little friend out from behind the TV stand and into his room. And there was no telling what Ma would do if she stumbled across it on her way to a hot bath. With that in mind, he had tossed what was left of the peanut butter sandwich under his bed and hoped to God it would follow the scent.

His mother was putting away some groceries, talking about the rudest customer she'd ever met; a guy in a dark suit and a wide brimmed hat, who'd come into the dinner acting like he stood five notches higher than everybody else. That was when the small TV Ma kept on the counter, the one she liked to watch the soap operas on while she made hamburger helper, flickered to life, all on its own. Her back was still turned when that smiling face appeared.

"Ra-row."

Kevin's hand found the plug and snapped it out of the socket.

"What'ya say honey?" his mother asked. She was on her tippy toes, trying to slide a box of dried pasta onto a top shelf in the pantry.

But the image on the TV was still there. Kevin looked down in disbelief at the plug in his hand.

His mother was starting to turn around when he snatched the whole thing off the kitchen counter.

"What in heaven's name are you doing?"

Kevin stopped and didn't dare turn around, for fear his mother would see the image.

"RA-ROW."

"Excuse me, young man?"

Kevin looked over his shoulder. "Sorry Ma, I was... practicing my Chinese. You know, harrow, how har you doowin."

"That isn't the least bit funny."

"Sorry," Kevin said.

"And what are you doing with my TV?"

"Must be on the fritz. Keeps showing static. I'll put it into the garage and take it to Steve's repair shop tomorrow."

Kevin was barely around the corner when the voice came again. "Rorry."

"Kevin, I'm warning you."

"Won't happen again, Ma. "

A few moments later, he returned to find his mother banging her cell phone against the palm of her hand. "Damndest thing, I have static on my cell phone too."

Ma laid it on the counter and looked over at Kevin.

"What is it? You've got that guilty look all over your face."

Kevin knew exactly what she was referring to.

"I haven't gone yet," he admitted. "I meant to, I really did, but..."

"Gone where? What are you talking about?"

"To the Olaks'. To return the…"

"Who are the Olaks? What on earth are you on about?"

"When you called today and you were super pissed and you said I had to go back–"

"Kevin you're scaring me. I never called you today. Heck, I was up to my eyeballs till well after lunch and for Chrix sake, I didn't even get a smoke break, much less time to call home and cuss you out over God knows what. Please tell me you and your friends haven't been sniffin' gas tanks. That stuff'll make you lose your mind. You'll end up like that guy in Florida, who started eating people's faces off."

Kevin's mouth was in the shape of a perfect 'o'. He'd been trying to say something for the last minute and a half, but no matter how hard he tried, nothing would come out.

10

But for Chrix sake, you're gonna get on your bike and bring back whatever it was that you stole. You do that and we'll forget this ever happened.

Kevin was stumbling up the stairs, his mind racing. The phone call he had received earlier today, when Ma had started tearing him a new one, was still echoing in his ears. But that hadn't been Ma, had it? They had sounded a lot like her. The way she said Chrix instead of Christ whenever she was really angry, as though somehow she wasn't technically taking the Lord's name in vain. The real question that kept circling back to him was: if that wasn't his Ma on the phone, then who was it?

Kevin had just reached the top riser when he saw that the door to his brother's room was ajar. Every so often, he would hear Ma sobbing quietly inside Jason's room. She wasn't the only one who missed him, but ever since his little brother's passing, he had felt an almost overwhelming need to stay strong. Mostly for her. He was all she had left.

Kevin nudged open the door and peeked inside. The room was empty. Nothing had been touched since the day Jason had taken that last trip to the hospital. Dust was collecting on the headboard of his bed and on his dresser, where he'd lined up his baseball trophies. Even the glass case where Jason kept the loose teeth that had fallen out, long after he stopped believing in the Tooth Fairy. Kevin leaned in closer. The case containing Jason's baby teeth was open. But that wasn't the strange part. The strange part was that the teeth had disappeared.

That was when Jason's pay-as-you-go cell phone, the one Ma had bought him before he got sick with the Leukemia, began to buzz and crackle. Kevin's pulse spiked. He knew exactly what was causing it, although he hadn't the faintest idea how it was being done. Jason's cell phone had been sitting on his night table for almost a year now. There was no way it had any kind of charge left in it, but that hadn't stopped Ma's television in the kitchen from coming to life, even after Kevin yanked the plug clear from the wall, had it? He inched towards it, at once certain he knew what face he would find looking back at him from the phone's tiny screen and also angry that it had ventured into a room that was considered out of bounds.

Kevin picked up the phone from the night table, but this time there was no face. Suddenly the static cut out and another noise took its place. A wet and disturbing sound like when you pull a drumstick off a cooked chicken. Kevin dropped down on one knee. He was going to peek under the bed and see what was there. Surely it was his little friend, but he hadn't the faintest clue what on Earth it was doing under there. Kevin was bending down when the entire bed bucked nearly a foot in the air. He jumped to his feet and fled his brother's old bedroom, slamming the door closed behind him.

A hand touched his shoulder and he screamed.
"You know you're not supposed to go in there."
He spun around to find his mother with an almost wounded expression on her face.

159

"I hope you didn't mess anything up." She went to move passed him, but he stayed in her way.

"Please Ma, I swear I didn't mess anything up. I left it just like it was." He was still breathing hard and hoping whatever was under the bed would stay quiet for just another few seconds.

"Frankly Kevin, I don't know what's gotten into you."

"I'm not sure either, Ma. Maybe I'm just feeling guilty for not finishing my paper route this morning. Maybe I should head off and get that all finished up."

"You will, young man, but first you're going to eat your supper."

-11-

Kevin sat down at the kitchen table. A single place had been set. Before him were two steaming Hot Pockets and a glass of milk.

Upstairs, Ma was soaking in a bath. He didn't mind eating on his own so much. Mostly because he knew Ma was rarely in a good mood until she'd 'washed her worries away', as she liked to put it. Though Kevin didn't quite understand how lying in a tub of scalding hot water did anything but give you second degree burns. His friend at school, Josh, said it had something to do with men-o-pause, but Kevin wasn't so sure it had anything to do with men. Men had been the cause of most of his mother's heartache. First, when Dad ran off and then soon after when Jason got sick. Now he was the only one left and more often than not, he felt like more of a burden to his mother than a source of pride and joy.

Kevin heard the footsteps descending the stairs and the first thought to cross his mind was:

This might be Ma's shortest bath ever.

But the sound of those feet didn't sound right at all. They sounded nothing like the way Ma lumbered down each step, as though the weight of the world were crushing her into the ground. There was a childlike gait to whoever was heading his way and for a distinct moment,

Kevin felt fear begin to surge in the pit of his belly. It was one of the Olaks. The little girl Paul had told him about. Somehow she had found a way in and was coming to collect whatever had come out of that giant acorn underneath his bed.

The sound of feet grew louder and Kevin held his breath. A second later a figure turned the corner.

Standing before him, naked as the day he was born, stood his brother. Jason lifted a hand and waved.

"Herrow Evin."

Kevin screamed and nearly fell out of his chair.

-12-

"Take a deep breath," Paul said, laying a hand on Kevin's shoulder. They were in Burt's Java Jungle and Paul was watching the strange looking boy sitting next to Kevin, as he stuck his index finger into a bottle of 7up and pulled it out with a plunk. Above him, Burt's brand new thirty inch Samsung was showing snowy static. "You wanna tell me what's got you so riled up?"

Kevin's hands were under the table, doing a wild jig. "I don't really know where to start."

"Why not try at the beginning."

Plunk

Paul and Kevin looked over at Jason who set the bottle of 7up back on the table. "Rorry."

"Who's your friend?" Paul asked.

"That's what I'm trying to tell you. He's not my friend. He's my brother, only…" Kevin's voice descended into a whisper. "My brother died a year ago."

Paul's eyes narrowed, his gaze flicking back between the two of them. "I don't understand. He doesn't look dead to me."

Kevin reached into his back pocket, removed his wallet, undid the Velcro strip and produced a dog eared piece of paper. It was a funeral card and it had Jason's picture on it.

163

"You remember that acorn I had, when you drove me home," Kevin was saying, "well it wasn't an acorn and I didn't exactly find it."

"Not an acorn…"

"No. It was some sort of pod and it fell under my bed and then this thing came out and the TV started talking to me and it ate a peanut butter sandwich…"

Paul's hands went up. "Whoa, whoa, whoa. Are you tailing me?"

"Tailing? You mean trolling? No, I swear to God, Mr. Roberts, this isn't a joke."

"*Irin't a roak.*" Jason repeated, as he emptied out all the sugar packets and piled the loose granules into a mound.

Kevin continued. "I don't know how to get him to stop. I found him in my brother's room and he stole one of his baby teeth. I didn't think much of it at first." Kevin pointed his thumb in Jason's direction. "Not until he came waltzing down the stairs."

"Where did you say you got that acorn again?"

"I didn't say. You know that family staying in the Alistair place?"

"The Olaks?"

"Yeah, them."

"*Yaw, rem.*"

"The basement floor was covered with the things. Hot as hell down there, too. What's wrong?" Kevin asked, noticing the sudden change in Paul's mood. "You look like you've seen a ghost."

"And you're sure it was the Olaks' house you were in?"

"Positive. Why?"

"*Rawsitive. Rye?*" Jason was leaning forward now, as though he too were a part of the conversation.

164

Paul took a deep breath and explained what he had found on the library microfiche and at the McGary family crypt.

"You saying the Olaks are ghosts?" Kevin blurted out incredulously.

Paul reached across the table and grabbed his arm. "Keep your voice down. No they're not ghosts." His eyes flickered over Jason and for some reason he didn't want to pull them away. "Whatever they are, they're somehow able to absorb DNA from the dead and make themselves look just like that person. In time, they might even take on their mannerisms. Maybe even their memories." A strange sort of thought was running through Paul's mind as he spoke and it had to do with snatching one or two of those eggs and heading straight for Pleasant view Cemetery, where his wife and son were buried.

"Everything all right Mr. Roberts?"

Kevin's voice snapped Paul back to reality.

"Has Jason...er I mean it, said anything yet, about who they are and where they're from?"

Kevin shook his head. "Not yet. So far all Jason does is repeat whatever I say. Watch this. Eat shit and die."

"Eeet rit n' rye," Jason said stoically.

Paul smiled. "Sounds like someone doing a bad Japanese accent."

"Yeah, that's what Ma said."

"You sort of think of him as your brother, don't you?"

"I don't know. Maybe I do."

"Is that why you don't want to give him back?"

"I don't know what they're gonna do if I give him back?" Kevin ran through the unusual phone call he received earlier and the fear he had experienced upon learning that it hadn't really been his mother on the other end of the line.

Paul's expression darkened. "If you keep him, you know what that'll mean, don't you?"

Kevin folded his arms. "No, what will it mean?"

Jason also folded his arms. "*Ro, rawt rill it meen?*"

"They're gonna come looking for him."

-13-

Paul had no sooner said the words when he noticed the man in the black suit at the other end of the coffee shop watching them. There was something about that man Paul didn't like, not one bit. Something he couldn't quite put his finger on.

The man in the dark suit got up, tossed a few dollars onto the table and was heading their way just as a young girl sauntered in from outside. She must have noticed Kevin and headed right for their table.

"Oh no," Kevin whispered. "It's Sally Fink. The biggest busybody in junior high."

"Hi Kevin," Sally said smiling past him at Jason. "Who's your frie…" Her hand shot up to her mouth. "Oh my God, he looks just like your brother. Oh, my heart's beating a million miles an hour. I thought I was seeing a ghost. Not that you're a ghost or anything."

Kevin smiled weakly. "His name's… Sigfried. He's my cousin, visiting from Germany."

"Oh, Sigfried, so nice to meet you."

Jason jabbed a finger up his nose and started digging around. "Ro Rigfeed, ro rice to reet you."

Sally's face dropped a notch or two, before she scurried away.

Paul did all he could to stifle a gale of laughter. "Sigfried?"

"Ma loves Sigfried and Roy and it's the only thing that came to me."

Jason put a hand to his own chest. "*Sigfried*," he said, nodding to emphasize the point.

"What's wrong Kevin?"

"It's gonna sound silly, but Jason used to pick his nose all the time and it would drive Ma crazy."

"You think he's becoming more and more like your brother, don't you?"

"Is that such a bad thing to want?"

Paul and Kevin were still feeling amazed by what they'd just witnessed, when the man in black approached them.

"Hello gentlemen. My name is Frank Santorelli and I'm a reporter for the National Enquirer. You folks haven't noticed anything strange around here lately, have you? The Enquirer's the top selling newspaper in the country as you probably know and we pay very, very well, let me assure you."

Paul frowned. "You asking us if we've seen any sparkly vampires or little green men?"

"No, I'm asking if you've seen anything... unusual."

"Yeah, as a matter of fact maybe I have." Paul leaned in, so did Frank Santorelli. "See there's this guy, oh, around your height and your weight, running around Shelby in the middle of summer with a black suit on, asking a lot of dumb questions. How's that for unusual?"

Frank tipped his hat. "Thanks for your time, gentlemen."

"Damn bloodsuckers," Paul spat, when he was sure the man was out of earshot.

"Ma mentioned a guy like that was in the dinner today, acting like a real jerk." Kevin glanced over at Jason and then back to Paul. "Do you think he knows?"

"Hard to say. For all we know he might even be one of them. But we got more important things to figure out. Like, what are we gonna do when the Olaks show up looking for good ol' Sigfried here?"

Kevin didn't say a word, but the fear on his face said he already knew.

-14-

A few minutes later the three of them were in Paul's Nissan, travelling at about thirty miles over the speed limit.

"I can't think of another option right now, can you?" Kevin said.

"But setting fire to the Alistair house," Paul shot back. "I mean, what if someone's inside?"

Kevin sat up straight, looking incredulous. "And what if those eggs all hatch and suddenly Shelby becomes infested with those things. We won't be able to tell the humans from the aliens."

Paul still didn't seem convinced. "You really believe they're aliens?"

"No doubt about it. Boxes with blinking lights and a basement filled with creatures that control electronics with their minds. Not to mention the way they can clone people. I don't know what you'd call that, but whatever they are, they aren't human. Except for Jason, that is."

Paul glanced in his rearview mirror and the neutral expression on Jason's face made him sigh. "I've got a five-gallon gas can in the trunk. I say we call the Olaks, tell them we have what they want and suggest they meet us over in the next town. Then when they're gone, we go inside and search the place."

"Sirch dah place," Jason said, wearing a Cheshire grin that looked more like a mask.

"Did you hear that?" Kevin shouted. "He's finally speaking English."

Jason mimicked Kevin again and this time it was almost spot on, except for the word English, which sounded more like ringlish.

"I wish Jason here could tell us where they came from and why they're here."

"How would he know?" Kevin shot back. "He only just hatched today."

Paul held the wheel with one hand while he fished his cell phone out of his front pocket with the other. When he found it he dialed a number and hit send.

"Hey Fred, listen I need–"

A pause and Kevin could hear a voice yammering on the other end.

"For God's sake I'm not a telemarketer. It's Paul. I need a favor. The Olaks have an account with you don't they? They only pay cash? Yeah, that makes sense. Well, I'm looking for a phone number for them. Did they keep the same number the Alistair's used to have? I didn't know that. Go ahead and give it to me, would you Fred?" Another pause as Paul made a one handed turn. "Thanks, appreciate it."

Paul hit end call and dialed in the number Fred had given him. Kevin watched Paul's brow furrow. No one was picking up. Jason was playing with the car windows, enthralled.

Then finally: "Mr. Olak? Don't worry about who this is. I understand you lost something of great value recently. If you want it back, you and your entire family will meet me in the Home Depot parking lot, on Sussex in Mayderville, in exactly one hour. You fail to show or you don't bring everyone with you, then you can forget ever seeing it again, whatever it is."

171

Paul disconnected and turned around to see Kevin with his hand over Jason's mouth.

Kevin smiled sheepishly. "I was worried he'd blurt something out. Hey, you think they fell for it?"

"We'll find out in the next five minutes."

-15-

Paul drove past the Olak house twice before pulling into the driveway. Their pickup truck was gone and the place looked as if it was locked up tight.

In the back seat, Kevin turned to Jason, who was still fiddling with the window button, even though it had stopped working when the car was turned off. "We're going inside for a minute. You stay here. Do you understand me?"

Jason tilted his head. "Sigfried stay here."

Kevin's face lit up. "You understand what I'm saying?"

Jason nodded.

"Your name is Jason, now."

"Jason now."

"No, just Jason."

"No, just Jason."

Kevin sighed. "Oh never mind. You stay here and we'll be right back."

Paul was already at the front door, rattling the handle, when Kevin came up behind him.

"Any luck?"

"Not yet. They've got one of those fancy computerized locking systems. We might need to just break a window." Paul's gaze drifted from the keypad on the door to a spot over Kevin's shoulder. "What's he doing here?"

Kevin turned to find Jason standing right behind him. "No Jason. Get back in the car." He turned to Paul in despair. "I told him like twenty times, he never listens."

"There isn't time to call Cesar Milan and have him house trained; if he wants to follow, let him follow. Why don't you head around back and see if there's another way in."

Paul's reference to that TV Dog Whisperer guy jogged something loose in Kevin's head. "You know that's probably it."

"What is it?"

"Jason hasn't been programmed. Not like the others have. Programmed for whatever horrible thing they've come here to do. He's a blank slate." Kevin was about to go, when he saw Jason reach a hand out and grasp the door handle. The numerical read-out on the keypad burst into life, rattling off numbers at a mile a minute. Suddenly the door popped open and Jason walked inside.

"Wait for us," Kevin cried.

As he entered, he was hit right away by a blast of hot air. The basement door was open. That was where Kevin had found the eggs and all three of them headed downstairs.

The basement was exactly how Kevin remembered it. The air heavy and tropical, the floor littered with tiny mounds, that at the time had looked like tennis balls. On the furnace was the electronic control box. He went up to it for a closer look and couldn't help noticing the strange markings. They looked like hieroglyphics.

But the other object Kevin spotted over by the furnace stopped him dead. A small, metallic cube that was pulsating in the rhythm of a heartbeat.

Paul must have noticed it too. "What is that?"

Even Jason was studying the glowing object. As Kevin picked it up, the pulsating light stopped.

"I haven't the foggiest."

"Maybe it's some kind of alien ashtray," Paul offered.

Kevin looked at him as though he had lost his mind.

Paul let out a dry laugh. "A famous astronomer named Neil Degrasse Tyson once told alien abductees that the next time they grab you, snatch an alien ashtray off a shelf when they're not looking. That way scientists would finally have some physical evidence." A smile spread across his face. "He was trying to ridicule them, of course. But it looks like we may have found our ashtray."

The cube was dark grey and no more than an inch long on each side.

"We just need to figure out how to make it glow again," Kevin said.

"Whoa, cowboy!" Paul cut in. "We don't even know what it does. I don't think we should be in such a hurry to get it working. Besides, we're here to search the place, not collect souvenirs."

Paul had barely finished speaking when Jason reached out and cupped the cube in the palm of his hand.

"Jason wai—" Kevin sputtered.

Almost at once the cube began to turn red and then white. A violent burst of light shot out from it and Paul grabbed hold of Kevin's shirt and dragged him closer. But the object hadn't exploded. The cube filled the dimly lit basement with a three dimensional image. Tiny specs of light, spinning around one another in tight clusters. Kevin's jaw hung open in awe.

"What is this?" Paul asked.

Kevin shook his head. "It looks like a star map."

In the center of the hologram, just below the basement's single hanging lightbulb, was what looked like a rather large binary system, filled with a series of Jupiter sized planets. Closer to the rotating stars was a smaller ball, with several moons and no oceans.

"The goldilocks zone," Kevin whispered.

"Huh," Paul said in a daze.

"Gosh, you don't ever watch the Discovery Channel, do you? The goldilocks zone is when a planet is just close enough to its sun to support life. A bit closer and it would bake. Any further out and it would freeze."

Suddenly the image shifted and began flickering through space at an awesome speed. Planets whizzed by, then entire solar systems. Then it slowed before a system that looked very familiar to Kevin and even Paul. A tiny blue ball surrounded by white vapor.

Earth.

Jason's eyes rolled up to the whites and he began babbling. Kevin's cell phone began making all kinds of weird noises and he didn't dare look, terrified of what he might see on the screen.

A glowing holographic face appeared before them. Kevin didn't think it looked human at all. More like something you'd see in the fish section of the supermarket. Soon, that strange face split into two. The two became four and four eight, until the entire three dimensional space was filled with the same expressionless face staring back at them.

"The Olaks are scouts," Kevin shouted.

The hologram faded and the cube returned to normal, as the room was plunged into darkness.

Jason's eyes had returned to normal too, but there was something different about him now. The glazed, vacant look from before was gone, replaced instead with brightness, intelligence.

Paul suddenly seemed concerned and Kevin couldn't blame him.

"What if something in the cube finally programmed Jason into becoming one of the Olaks?" Paul asked and without even waiting for an answer he turned to leave.

"Where you going?"

"I've seen enough," he replied. "You were right. Let's torch the place."

Paul ran up the stairs.

Slowly, Kevin turned to Jason.

"Jason?" he said in a whisper.

Jason turned his head. "Yes?"

"Are you all right?" he asked, feeling stupid for asking such a lame question.

"I'm fine. How are you?"

"Scared," Kevin replied.

"What frightens you?"

Kevin paused and took a step back. "I guess I'm worried you're…I mean, I hope you're not, but…well, are you one of them now?"

Paul returned with the gas can and started pouring it over the floor.

"One of who?" Jason replied.

"An alien," Paul blurted out.

Jason turned to him and Paul stopped dousing the floor for a moment.

"I'm not sure what I am," Jason said.

"You're not gonna try and hurt us now, are you?" Kevin asked, feeling stupid for asking a question that made him sound like a total suck ass.

Jason shook his head.

Paul ran his free hand through his hair. "That cube clearly did something to him."

"Maybe you were right. It downloaded something into his brain. Go on Paul, ask him a question."

Paul cleared his throat. "Where are you from?"

Jason's eyes began to flutter, as though he were reading a teleprompter, projecting from his skull. "Our

177

home has two suns and many moons. My people once lived in the sea, but many years ago we began slowly moving onto the land and breathing the air. Air very much like your own."

"Is that why you're here?" Kevin asked. "Because our planets are so similar?"

Jason nodded. "There are so few blue jewels within reach. Our people have studied you for many years, through interstellar optics. It has only been recently that we've had the means to make the trip in person."

"But why?"

"To spread out among you. To study. To learn."

"Learn what?" Kevin asked.

"Everything we can."

"And then, when you've learned everything you can?"

His eyes were still fluttering. "We must replicate until every facet of the human experience has been observed and recorded."

"Your people gather information," Kevin said. "Oh my God, you're cosmic librarians."

"But what about us? If you keep multiplying, what happens to the humans already living here? There's barely enough room here for us as it is."

"On every planet we've found, the indigenous population does not survive the period of replication."

"No shit they don't," Kevin spat. He couldn't believe what he was hearing. The end of the human race.

Paul was giving him a scolding look.

"Oh, I'm sorry for cussing, but come on Paul. Jason's talking about the end of bike riding and ice cream on hot, sunny days. The end of summer ball games and pulling your sister's hair. You gotta cut me a bit of slack."

"Why do you need to destroy the very thing you're studying, I don't understand?" Paul asked.

Jason's head tilted back. "I don't have the answer to that question. That is the way it has always been done. But are we all that different?"

"Hell yeah," Kevin replied. "We humans don't break everything we study. Most of it we let live in cages and stuff. Look at Marine Land and Zoos…"

"Kevin, you're not helping."

Kevin bit his lip.

Paul was about to ask another question when Jason's eyes stopped fluttering and returned to normal. Almost as if he'd woken up. But it was the next thing Jason said that made chills run up Kevin's spine.

"Someone else is in the house."

-16-

The three of them raced up to the main floor, taking the steps two at a time. Paul was tilting the gas can as they went, leaving a trail they could light from the front door.

When Kevin and Paul reached the front door, they realized Jason wasn't with them.

Then they heard a sound from upstairs. Footsteps.

"Jason," Kevin cried out and it almost sounded like a question. He went around the corner and found the staircase. Kevin's pulse was beating a wild rhythm in his throat. A sense of terrible fear was clawing up his back, but he fought the urge to run and willed his feet upwards, step by step. Every creak nearly deafened him.

Paul was right behind him, admonishing him to leave before the Olaks came home.

When they reached the top riser, Kevin spotted a bedroom, the door slightly ajar and even from here Kevin could see a jumble of lights flashing inside.

A second later, Kevin and Paul were standing before a room on the second floor of the Olak house, every fiber of their beings coursing with disbelief. Before them was a woman – Mrs. Olak? – and she wasn't wearing any clothes. Her body was attached to some kind of chrome colored machine that straddled the bed. Just past the doorway was Jason, standing as rigid as a mannequin in a

180

storefront window. The machine hunched over the woman was a box filled, with pulsating lights; protruding from either end, like a series of giant tentacles, were long slippery arms that were attached to Mrs. Olak's private parts. She seemed to be in some kind of trance and the first thought that fired through Kevin's mind had to do with the strange devices Ma kept in her top drawer. The vibrating ones that made her really, really angry whenever he brought them up over dinner. Except this was somehow different. This looked a lot less like Mrs. Olak was pleasuring herself and a lot more like she was about to give birth.

Then Jason started to speak in a language Kevin had never heard before. It sounded like gibberish, like he was reciting streams of meaningless words; the way those people sometimes did at church when the holy spirit took hold of them. Paul was calling from behind him but he might as well have been a million miles away. "We have to get out of here." There was more than a touch of terror in his voice, which helped to snap Kevin out of his trance.

He reached out and grabbed Jason's arm; the cell phone in Kevin's left pocket began to ring, but ringing wasn't really the right word to describe it. It was kicking up a fierce racket, as though his mother knew what he was up to and her anger was somehow audible. He plucked it out and the twisted face he saw looking back at him on the screen made his stomach lurch. It wasn't his mother's face he saw. It was Mrs. Olak, and it wasn't the face she wore to look human, but her real face. The face of a monster.

Kevin yanked at Jason's arm, trying to pull him from the room.

They were nearly out, when Kevin caught a final glance of Mrs. Olak. He noticed that her eyes had snapped open and she was glaring at him; all the blood in his veins turned to concrete. She had woken up and was now scrambling to tear the machine from her naked body and Kevin heard himself scream. A second later, Paul grabbed him and all three of them fled, Jason still reciting gibberish as they bolted towards the front door.

All of them froze when they saw Mr. Olak and his daughter, the one with the dazzling eyes, running up the porch steps outside towards them.

-17-

Paul slammed the front door shut.

"Kevin," he shouted, "slide me over one of those chairs from the kitchen."

Mr. Olak was rattling the knob, trying to push his way in. Kevin grabbed one of the chairs and ran over to where Paul was struggling to keep the door shut.

The little Olak girl ran across the porch. It looked like she was heading around the back of the house.

"Close that back door and fast," Paul yelled, sending Kevin scurrying through the kitchen, as he wedged the chair under the front door handle and only letting go when he was sure it would hold against Mr. Olak's onslaught.

That was when Paul heard the footsteps on the stairs. Someone was coming down and he sure as hell didn't need to look to know it was Mrs. Olak, stark naked and looking mightily pissed off. The skin on her face looked loose, as though she were wearing a sick kind of human mask. She ambled down the first few steps, her legs bowed out from the birthing machine she'd been attached to for God knows how long, giving her walk an eerie, inhuman quality.

But as Paul watched her struggle down those stairs, her eyes caught hold of his and the sense of urgency and utter horror that he had felt piercing his insides like a hot knife, suddenly began to waver. Her eyes looked somehow bottomless, almost beautiful and Paul found himself swimming in their depths. They were communicating with him, in a way he didn't quite understand or explain, and Mrs. Olak's powerful gaze was telling him to remove the chair from under the doorknob. It seemed like such a wonderful idea at the time too, and Paul was dimly aware of his hands reaching down and grasping the lacquered kitchen chair by the rim.

He was about to yank it free and open the door so Mr. Olak could come in…and take care of each of them in turn… when Paul heard a terrible screech.

He turned back just in time to see Jason charge up the stairs and tackle Mrs. Olak, pushing her over the railing. The two of them went tumbling onto a table containing a vase and a portable phone, crushing it all into a heap of splinters and glass underneath them.

And just like that, the spell was broken. Paul jammed the chair back under the door and ran to make sure Jason was okay.

A second later Kevin was by his side.

Jason had fallen on top of Mrs. Olak, who wasn't moving. There was a deep gash in her head, but instead of blood, a strange black liquid oozed from the wound.

She wasn't the only one bleeding, Jason was too, the same blackish goo. It was running down his face and Kevin went to wipe it away.

"Don't," Paul said, grasping his hand. "We don't know what that is. It could have some kind of alien bacteria, or worse."

The two of them pulled Jason to his feet. Kevin glanced down at Mrs. Olak. "You think she's dead?"

"I'm not sure, but we need to find something to tie her up with, in case she isn't."

Kevin freed one of his hands and undid his belt. "Will this do?"

A minute later, Jason was standing on his own and Mrs. Olak's arms were tied to the banister. Kevin and Paul stood before her, beltless.

Mr. Olak wasn't by the front door anymore. Kevin ran to check the back door and returned a moment later. "They're not there."

A buzzing sound from the kitchen made them all turn at once.

The television set had turned itself on and it was showing white, snowy static; it was clear, even from a distance, that a face was slowly taking shape. A hideous face, that didn't look human at all. The image slowly became clearer and so too did its disturbing features. Deep, sunken eyes, skin that was moist and grey; it reminded Kevin of the octopus he'd seen once, in Tom's fish market. Small tentacles wiped around the mouth as the face glared back and forth.

"They're looking for us," Kevin whispered, ducking down. "Trying to figure out where we are in the house, so they can attack where we least expect it."

"Paul," Kevin said, trying to keep his voice down. "Can you reach the plug for the TV?"

Paul shook his head. "Not without it seeing me, no."

The face on the screen was still searching, its cavernous black eyes wide, as the tentacles around its mouth flailed to and fro.

"Don't look into its eyes," Paul said.

Kevin looked up at him, suddenly hopeful. "I have an idea." He dropped down onto his stomach and crawled, army style, into the kitchen. When he reached the counter, he used the edge to pull himself up, plugged the sink and turned on the tap. Slowly it began to fill, but the face on the TV must have heard the noise of the running water because now it was looking down at Kevin and the boy was doing everything in his power to avoid staring into those Medusa-like eyes.

When Kevin looked behind him, Paul was mouthing the words "What the hell are you doing?"

"Trust me," Kevin mouth back.

The sink was nearly half full when Kevin reached up, turned off the tap and rose to his full height. Now the face could see him clearly, but in another second or two that wouldn't really matter. Kevin heaved the small TV off the kitchen counter and into the sink. An explosion of sparks shot out, nearly blinding him. A second before the screen blew out, Kevin saw that distorted alien face, Mr. Olak's *real* face, screaming in pain. Then the entire house seemed to let out a moan before all the power went out

Kevin's suspicion had been right. When these bastards merged with electronics, a part of them was somehow actually in the damn thing.

"Did you kill him?" Paul asked.

"I don't know. How's Jason?" but even from here Kevin could see his brother was bracing himself against the wall, groggy and sluggish from the tumble he had taken over the railing.

In the basement, the sound of breaking glass made them all freeze. One of the Olaks had broken in and they were shuffling around downstairs in the dark.

Kevin wasn't sure which of them was down there, but they were about to get one hell of a surprise. He opened a drawer looking for a knife and found it empty. Paul was beside him in a second, searching for some kind of weapon, but all the cupboards were bare. Even the fridge was empty, as though they were in some kind of twisted dolls' house.

It was charging up the stairs

All three of them grabbed hold of any kind of weapon they could find. Paul had yanked a drawer clean off its castors while looking for something he could use, and was now holding it over his head, ready to crush the skull of whatever came through the door.

The door swung open and before them, stood the man in the black suit they'd seen in Burt's Java Jungle.

"Hold your fire, boys," he said, his hands in the air as though he were under arrest. One of them slid down and into his breast pocket, from which he pulled a wallet. He flipped it open, revealing a strange looking badge with a picture of the planet Earth covered by what looked like a web.

NASA?

That was Kevin's first thought.

"My name isn't Frank Santorelli. I'm Agent Keller," the man said. "I'm here to get you out."

"B-but the Olaks are out there," Kevin stuttered.

"They're on the second floor, coming in through an upstairs window as we speak."

"And how do we know you're not one of them?"

"Because if I was, you'd already be dead. Now, in another minute this entire house is gonna look like a gaping hole in the ground. So you can come with me, or stay. The choice is yours."

Paul blinked and headed for the front door.

"Not that way," Agent Keller snapped. "We can't risk anyone knowing you were inside. This way." And he led all three of them down to the basement.

Kevin was taking the stairs two at a time, holding his nose against the heavy smell of gasoline, not entirely sure if they were being led into a trap. That's when he heard the muffled sound of footsteps coming from upstairs.

"Hurry up," Keller shouted.

They were heading across the basement, toward the broken window. The same one Kevin had used to escape after stealing the egg. Kevin glanced down. The floor was still littered with them, making it hard to run.

Kevin was the first to crawl out, careful to avoid the sharp bits of glass that remained along the edge of the window frame. Then came Agent Keller. Paul was getting ready to climb out the narrow opening when the door behind him swung open.

"Oh God, hurry," Kevin shouted.

The stress must have gotten to Paul, because his hand slipped, the glass carving a deep gash in his palm. Kevin and Agent Keller both reached in, took one of Paul's hands and yanked him out. Paul was by no means overweight. In fact, for a man his age, he was quite thin, but for Kevin, it felt like Paul weighed a thousand pounds. And all he could think about was Jason. As Paul cleared the window, Kevin could see Mr. Olak, or at least what he thought was Mr. Olak, since the human face he used to fool people had completely vanished.

Kevin and Agent Keller each grabbed hold of Jason's hands and started to pull. He didn't make it past his chest before he began to be sucked back inside. Mr. Olak had grabbed hold of Jason's legs and it was clear that he was much stronger than the two of them combined.

"I don't think I can hold him anymore," Kevin said, tears welling up in his eyes. Paul tried to help too, but it was no use. Blood was gushing from Paul's palm as he tried to hold on.

"Twenty seconds," Keller said. "We don't have time."

"Twenty seconds until what?" Kevin spat. He wasn't going to give up.

Keller looked dead serious. "Trust me, you don't want to find out."

That's when Kevin caught Jason's eye. They were bottomless, like two pools of impossibly deep water. Kevin was suddenly very calm.

"Let go, Kevin," Jason said. "It's time to let go."

As if in a dream, Kevin watched his hands release their grip and felt Jason's fingers slip through his as his brother was sucked back into the house. Kevin had lost him again and the pain struck him with all the raw power of a blow to the gut.

Keller and Paul were pulling Kevin away, out toward a grove of trees that ran parallel to the farm house. It was from there that they would eventually make their way to the road and the crowd of townspeople and firemen that had begun to assemble.

Keller looked at his watch and said: "It's on its way."

Kevin stopped and looked up just in time to see what looked like a blinding flash of lightning strike the roof of the Alistair house, dead center. An explosion of white hot sparks flew into the air and almost as if in response, fire shot out of the top floor windows, cascading down as it ignited the gasoline inside.

Soon they made it to the road and the group of onlookers who had gotten out of their cars to gawk. By then, the house had been hit for a third time and was completely engulfed in flames. Kevin couldn't hold back the tears anymore and collapsed into Paul's arms, sobbing.

-18-

Six months later

Kevin drove his scooter up the driveway and killed the engine. The newspaper sack tied behind his seat was empty. His daily deliveries were now completed in record time and Kevin still couldn't help but marvel at his new baby. She was black, with a lightning bolt struck across her side. That was Paul's idea. In fact, the scooter itself had been Paul's gift. Of course, Paul hadn't been able to be there in person. Shortly after the Alistair place was leveled, razed to the ground, he'd finally put aside the novel that had slowly been torturing him and started something new. A science fiction book, about aliens invading a small town. Against all odds, the novel had gone on to become a national bestseller.

It wasn't long after that the checks had started arriving, with the same hand written note every time.

Couldn't have done it without you!

Love,
Paul

Not quite enough to buy a mansion, but more than enough for his mother to stop worrying, for once in her life.

He was just glad she didn't know the half of it. Somewhere between the third lightning strike and the Alistair house tumbling into a heap, Agent Keller had up and vanished. Kevin had spent hours on the internet afterward, trying to figure out what branch of the government he worked for and what exactly had struck the house. It hadn't been long before he found a video on Youtube, in which Ronald Reagan addressed the UN, wondering how quickly the world might come together if faced with an alien threat from beyond Earth. And it had been around that time that he had started the Star Wars program. Kevin now knew that Star Wars had been about far more than protecting Americans from the Russians.

But knowing this didn't seem to ease Kevin's greatest pain. He missed Jason. Missed him more deeply than he could ever have imagined. The image of Jason's fingers slipping through his often played against the back of his eyes as he fell asleep, and again every morning when he awoke.

"Kevin," his mom called out, as he charged in the front door.

"Yeah, Ma."

She came to him holding a chocolate cake.

"Oh, thanks Ma."

"This isn't for you," she admonished. "I want you to take this next door."

"No one lives next door, Ma. The Darnesbys moved out months ago, after the bank foreclosed on their house."

"Yes, I'm well aware of that Kevin, there's a new family that's just moved in. They're definitely not from around here, I can tell by their strange accent, but this little offering should make them feel welcomed. Besides, it's the neighborly thing to do."

Kevin took the cake and headed for the door, not able to completely shake the strange little voice in his head. He hoped that the new neighbors would be nice. But more than that, he hoped they would be human.

LAST CALL

Although you're reading this story after Bird of Prey, this was the first tale I'd written about Buck and Tommy. I imagined them as a couple of lumberjacks with forearms the size of elephant trunks (which I came to learn, during a trip to Thailand, were pure slabs of muscle that could squeeze a man until his head popped off). I'd always wanted to write a scary story set in Alaska. There's something wild and untamed about the north that scares me; if it scares me, it means that maybe, hopefully, it will scare you too. But another important theme present here (and in some of my other work) is claustrophobia. I think any horror story needs a healthy dose of it in order to work.

Tommy "The Tank" Hodgkins stood staring out at the blowing drifts of snow. He had been thinking about closing the bar for over an hour now and in that time he had seen the weather outside go from nasty to downright dangerous.

The voice to his left startled him.

"You're not thinking about Buck again, are you?"

Tommy turned, so lost in thought, he had forgotten all about Allan, sitting not four feet away. The same spot he sat in nearly every night, sipping the tail end of a warm beer with his good hand. Allan's other hand was a metal hook; he poked it into the peanut jar and began fishing for nuts.

"Been well over a year now, Tommy," Allan said. "I ain't trying to be harsh or nothing, but Buck's not coming back. And that's a fact." A single peanut skittered out of his metallic grasp and fell to the floor.

"A year ago tonight," Tommy barked and Allan's head snapped up from his peanuts. "That's when it happened. Not over a year, not six years. A year ago - tonight. Buck wasn't just my boss, he was like a father to me and he was a damn good friend to you too, Allan."

The sting made Allan jerk his head up and the rolls of fat beneath his chin became visible for the first time. "Look Tommy, I'm just saying that people disappear without any kinda trace all the time. Cut and run is what they call it. In all the years I've been coming here, Lucky Lonie's has never turned a profit. And the old man probably knew you'd give him an ear full for being a coward. Hell, the police were all over this place and even they said nothing funny had happened."

Yes, Tommy remembered the police, and in customary Anchorage P.D. fashion, they had proven themselves about as useless as tits on a rooster. Looking at the receipts for that night, it was clear that the bar had been empty between eight and ten. Then, somewhere around eleven, about the time Buck would have been preparing to close down and call it a night, someone had come in. That someone had ordered a Blood Clot. Lucky Lonie's wasn't one of those fancy bars like in Anchorage, so Buck had put it through as a double Screwdriver. But the cops knew what the drink had really been, because someone had written the mix on the inside of a dirty napkin.

Blood Clot
1oz. Southern Comfort
½ oz. Grenadine
7up

The writing on that napkin had looked as though someone had grabbed a pen in a bunched up fist and just started scratching away. And whenever Tommy thought of Buck now, an image of that dirty napkin was almost all he ever saw.

"You better not start about that napkin again," Allan said, as though he could see the ghostly white square dancing behind Tommy's eyes.

Tommy took the peanut dish behind the bar and filled it up. Discussing the matter with Allan was like riding a merry go round. You spun round and round in circles until one person got a punch in the face. But there were things the police found that night that even Allan didn't know about. Things Tommy had never mentioned. Maybe in part because Allan would never have accepted the implication of those things, but mostly because he wasn't sure if he could accept them himself.

As far as Allan was concerned, Buck had disappeared without a trace; but that wasn't entirely true, was it? The police, in their bumbling fashion, had dismissed it, but on a patch of the mahogany bar, where Buck normally liked to stand and watch things, there had been a pool of saliva. And on either side was what had looked to Tommy like two handprints, gouge marks really, as if Buck had held on for dear life as someone had tried to wrench all two hundred and sixty three pounds of him out from behind the bar.

That unsettling thought was slowly stirring within him again.

If it could throw Buck around like a child's toy, what on earth could it do to me?

Allan was still blathering when the CB radio behind the bar went off. Allan stopped suddenly. The sound of heavy static and then the faint echo of a voice. "This is Sheriff Howard. Anyone there, over?"

Tommy plucked the mic of the stand. "Sheriff, this is Tommy Hodgkins. Go ahead."

"Tommy, we're getting word from Anchorage of a big storm heading your way. Advise you call it a night, over."

"Yeah, no shit," Allan said, looking outside as he killed the rest of his beer in a single gulp.

Tommy glanced at the clock on the wall and saw that it was approaching eleven. "Way ahead of you Sheriff. Over and out." Tommy hung the mic up.

Allan was standing now, albeit a little unsteadily. He shrugged awkwardly into his heavy winter parka before he stumbled towards the door.

He stopped. "You want me to wait?"

Tommy snatched up Allan's dirty glass and peanut dish and shook his head. "Don't bother. I won't be long."

For a reason that Tommy couldn't quite put his finger on, the sound of Allan's '83 Riviera, rumbling noisily to life and pulling away left him with an uneasy feeling. A trapped kind of feeling.

Outside, the snow was settling against the windows. The lights flickered and Tommy held his breath for the moment he was pitched into darkness. The night in the middle of nowhere wasn't at all like city dark. In the city, when it was dark, you could still find your way around, still get to where you were going. Country dark was so black that it felt like your eyes had been stabbed with hot pokers.

Tommy was in the middle of wiping down the bar-top, getting ready to flick off the tacky neon Budweiser sign over the jukebox and call it a night, when the door opened. An arctic gust flew in with an accompanying flurry of snow and slapped him in the face. He turned away for a moment, eyes watering, his pulse quickening. In from the pilling snow walked a figure wrapped from head to foot. Not a patch of skin was exposed and the sight made Tommy think of an old black and white movie he'd seen as a child: The Invisible Man.

Perched atop the figure's head and shoulders were tiny mountains of powdery snow. He shook himself free of it and stamped his feet against the wooden floor, his stout winter boots booming. An inexplicable sense of dread was clawing into Tommy's throat and he quickly chased it down with a shot of Jim Bean, heat spreading in his belly.

The stranger unwrapped his face and stepped forward into the light. He was a diminutive man with fine features and a long pointed nose. By the looks of him, Tommy guessed he hadn't shaved in a week or two. The man's hair, wet with snow, hugged the narrow confines of his head.

197

"Real killer out there," the man said and when his lips rose into a friendly, warm smile, Tommy could see that his eyes were deathly still. They were piercing eyes. The kind that could look right into your soul. Tell what you were thinking. Tommy found himself lost in those strange eyes and with the force of will he drew his attention back to the bar and the wet cloth in his hand.

"A-as a matter of fact," Tommy stammered. "I was just about to shut her down for the night." He offered the man the kind of weak smile that the waitress at Ted's Diner might offer, fresh out of hot apple pie; all the while trying to ignore the chilled feeling settling once again in his belly.

The man approached the bar. "I'm sure you could make an exception just this once... on account of the weather and all."

Tommy could hear a voice that sounded a lot like Buck's, urging him to say no, screaming against every logical part of his...

"Just the one," Tommy heard himself say from far away, only dimly aware he had just made a terrible mistake. "What'll it be then?"

The man's eyes narrowed. "Blood Clot."

Tommy's jaw fell open and nearly smacked the edge of the bar. His legs became gelatin. His arms turned to lead and he had to prop a shaky, numb hand against the bar to keep from falling over.

"Mister, looks like you just seen somethin' awful."

A part of Tommy was ready to bolt right there and then, jacket or no jacket—and take his chances with the biting cold and the snow and the wolves.

Then he scolded himself for letting a man half his size give him the heebie-jeebies.

Tommy glanced at the weather outside and for a second, he swore the driving snow didn't want him to leave, that it meant to bury him in here with...

The stranger's eyes were smiling now, but to Tommy there was something predatory about them. The man seemed to be sizing him up. The way a hyena might size up a lion cornered against the edge of a cliff.

Tommy's hand slipped beneath the bar and came to rest on the highly polished chestnut stock of the shotgun he kept there. B.S. was still carved on the hilt: Buck's initials. There had never been cause to use it against a customer before. He hoped to keep it that way.

The man had taken a napkin from the bar and was concentrating on scribbling something. His left hand grasped the pen in an awkward straight handed hold, and it reminded Tommy of his childhood. The stiff way his GI Joe action figures used to hold their toy guns. The man finished and slid the napkin across the bar, but Tommy didn't need to look at it to know what he had written.

"Guessin' you ain't never heard of it down in these parts," the man said tapping the napkin and right away Tommy could feel the lie in his voice.

"Can't say that I have." He glanced down at the scrawl and the very act of seeing it made the skin around his testicles retract painfully. He tried to swallow and had to fight to make it go down, his saliva sticking in his dry throat. "Not from around here, are you?" Tommy asked.

"Name's John Smith." The man reached out with one of his hands and Tommy took it. It was the rough hand of a mountaineer. "From north of here. Quite a ways. Here on business."

John Smith, Tommy thought skittishly. *Right. And who's your sister, Pocahontas?*

"You must be in some hurry, to risk driving around in this." He motioned to the window, now half-buried with snow and realization struck him that he hadn't seen the customary glare of headlights before the man had come in. Nor had he heard an engine. He recalled again

199

how the man's clothes had been weighed down with snow. Could he have been on foot? On foot in the middle of nowhere?

Tommy's hand felt for the gun again, but this time, it didn't put his mind at ease.

"If you don't mind my asking, what sort of business brings you our way?"

"At the moment," the man said, his eyes dropping, then returning to Tommy's. "You might say I'm in education."

Tommy peeled his hand away from the shotgun and fumbled for the grenadine, his nervous gaze never far from the stranger sitting before him.

"I sell books to elementary schools," John Smith was saying. "Pull in a percentage of whatever I manage. Easy part is passing off the Judy Blooms and the Lemony Snickets. The real trick is convincin' em to buy the stuff those little shits should really be reading. Dracula. Little Red Riding Hood. Kinda stuff those glorified librarians turn their prissy little noses up at."

A trail of saliva dribbled from the corner of the man's mouth and he wiped it away with the back of his hand and a look that might have passed for embarrassment.

Tommy fell dead silent.

"You ever read that one?" John Smith asked him.

The lights flickered again, but both men's eyes never wavered.

"Which story?"

"Little Red Riding Hood."

"Maybe, sure. When I was a kid."

"It's a true story."

"That so?" Tommy said, feigning interest when all he really wanted to do was get the hell out of there.

"Happened to a friend of mine—"

"Where'd you say you was from again? Fairbanks?" There was a heavy trace of fear on Tommy's lips now and the man's nose seemed to twitch at the scent.

"North of here. Quite a ways."

"Parts don't get much more north than this."

"There are places. More secluded. Fewer people. Less now than before. Which is why I've decided to give this place a shot. Forced migration you might say."

"So you can sell your books?"

The corner of the man's mouth quivered and then grew still. "That's right."

Tommy gripped the man's drink tightly in his hand. His knuckles were the color of raw chicken.

"Which part?" Tommy asked.

The man's eyes were on the drink in Tommy's hand. "Huh?"

"That friend of yours you mentioned."

This time, in Tommy's mind at least, the brown-out seemed to last for an eternity. And in that moment of darkness, Tommy was sure he had heard a gurgle coming from the back of the man's throat. Something low and terrifying…

"Little Red Riding Hood. You said it happened to a friend of yours."

"He was shot."

"Beg your pardon?"

The man smiled and in the dim pools of light around the bar, his face seemed different. Longer. Hairier. As though his face was beginning to charge shape entirely.

"My friend was shot."

"What does that have to do with Little Red–"

That gurgling sound again, but louder this time.

"He was shot dead by a man who worked for the lumber mill." The stranger's lips barely parted as he spoke, but it was enough for Tommy to see a mouthful of crooked, needle-sharp teeth that definitely hadn't been

201

there before. "A lumberjack you might say. Except before he was shot, he had already eaten the girl, bones and all."

The lights went out completely, plunging them both of them into a darkness so complete it felt to Tommy like his eyes had been scratched out. That low gurgling grew into a growl and then a deafening roar.

Tommy "The Tank" Hodgkins came up with the shotgun. Initials BS.

Outside, a flash of white light could be seen through the front window, half caked with snow.

Outside, the wind whipped against the door, drowning out the sound of ripping flesh. The thick blanket of snow lay on the ground, muffling, insulating. Drowning out the screams.

Also by Griffin Hayes

Novels
Malice
Dark Passage

Novellas
Hive I
Hive II
Hive III (coming soon!)
Bird of Prey
The Neighbors

Short Stories
The Second Coming
The Grip
Fatherland

Collections
Night Terror
Nightfall